THE ENCHANTED BUNGALOW

THE MYSTERY HOUSE SERIES, BOOK NINE

Eva Pohler

Eva Pohler Books
20011 Park Ranch
San Antonio, Texas 78259
www.evapohler.com

Publisher's Note: This is a work of fiction. Names, characters, places, and incidents are a product of the author's imagination. Locales and public names are sometimes used for atmospheric purposes. Any resemblance to actual people, living or dead, or to businesses, companies, events, institutions, or locales is completely coincidental.

Copy Editor: Alexis Rigoni

Book Cover Design by B Rose DesignZ

THE ENCHANTED BUNGALOW/ Eva Pohler. -- 1st ed.
Paperback ISBN: 978-1-958390-60-3

Contents

With gratitude to author Eleanor Phillips Brackbill whose book The Queen of Heartbreak Trail: The Life and Times of Harriet Smith Pullen, Pioneer Woman *supplied important historical information to my story.*

CHAPTER ONE

Ellen's Big Fail

Ellen touched the tip of her paintbrush to the canvas to add texture to the landscape and then stood back from the painting to have a look.

Before she could decide whether her work was done, her cell phone rang. It was Sue.

"We have a problem," Sue began. "Where are you? I'm at your front door, and no one's answering."

"In the studio out back. What's happened?" Ellen rushed to her backyard gate, her little dog, Moseby, following.

"You stay here," she said to her dog.

He lowered his head and obeyed.

Sue marched up Ellen's drive, moving faster than Ellen had seen her move in quite some time.

"What's happened?" Ellen asked again. "Are you alright? Your feet seem better."

"They are. Thanks for noticing. I'm just fine. You might not be able to tell it, but I've lost nearly thirty pounds for this trip."

"The foot surgery was such a good idea. You look fantastic."

"Well, it may have been for nothing, because Tanya is going to kill us."

Ellen screwed up her face. "What are you talking about?"

"Well, for one thing," Sue explained irritably, "you never made our room reservations."

Ellen cocked her head to the side. "What do you mean? I thought you were taking care of it?"

Sue shook her head. "I was in charge of the flights. You said you would book the rooms. I just called Oceanside in La Push to let them know about our late check in this Saturday, and they have no reservation for us—not in your name, not in my name, not in Tanya's name, and not even in Brian's name."

"You said you were taking care of the arrangements, Sue. I swear. Don't you remember? I said I would . . ." Ellen covered her mouth. "Oh, no."

"We're screwed," Sue said. "Oceanside is completely booked. I checked Forks and every town within an hour's drive. There are no places to stay. Tanya will be so disappointed. This is a disaster. It's her sixtieth, Ellen. I don't understand how you could forget to do something so important. And we've been talking about it for months."

Ellen would have cried if Moseby hadn't yipped at her. He didn't like to be excluded.

"Come inside." Ellen beckoned to Sue. "I'll figure something out."

Ellen led Sue through the backyard gate and into the house, and Moseby followed. The little black, curly-haired Doodle was part miniature poodle and part dachshund. He was a rescue Brian had seen a few months ago on Facebook. The post by a local shelter had said that the dog would be put down in twenty-four hours. Brian hadn't been able to resist the chance to save him and had adopted the dog for himself, but Moseby had imprinted on Ellen and had quickly become her baby.

She and Brian had just returned from a trip to the Maldives, and Ellen had asked him what they would do with the dog when they traveled. To her surprise, he had shown her a cloth pooch carrier she could wear like a crossbody purse.

"Moseby fits right here and can go anywhere with us," he had proclaimed proudly.

"And why Moseby?" she had asked. "Why not Snoopy or Shakespeare?"

His face had sobered a little. "Because Dan Moseby was my sidekick in the eighties, the best friend I ever had. He was killed in a hunting accident."

Ellen had jumped to her feet and had sandwiched the dog between them. "And now *this* Moseby. will be your new sidekick and best friend. Won't you, Moseby-Mo?"

Brian had grinned. "Moseby-Mo. I like that."

Unfortunately, Moseby was Ellen's sidekick through and through.

"Can I get you something to drink?" Ellen asked Sue as they passed through the kitchen.

"I've got a cherry coke in the car."

Mo danced in front of Sue, causing her to stop short.

"You must like me," Sue said to Moseby.

"He wants to go between your legs. It's just something he does. If you let him through, he'll settle down."

Sue laughed. "Well, I don't let just anyone between my legs."

Ellen giggled. "That's not what I heard."

"Well, you heard right." Sue let Mo run through her legs, and then he jumped onto the back of Ellen's chair.

"I can't believe I dropped the ball on this," Ellen said of the hotel reservations she forgot to make.

"Tanya will be so disappointed when we tell her we can't do it on her actual birthday. The soonest they can take us isn't until August when the whales are no longer active. And our flights are non-refundable."

They were supposed to fly out this Saturday—the Saturday before Mother's Day. It was Tuesday.

"I'll find a way, Sue. I promise."

Sue didn't look convinced as she sat on Ellen's couch. Ellen took a seat in her favorite chair, where she kept her laptop nearby. Despite the gold and the oil money, not to mention Brian's billions, Ellen's home and furnishings were rather modest. She spent her money on traveling, renovations, and eating out, and a good chunk of it went to her three kids and grandkids.

Moseby repositioned onto Ellen's shoulder.

"Does he think he's a cat?" Sue asked of the dog.

Ellen grinned. "Either that or a parrot."

"He's got some strange habits for a dog. Running between legs and sitting on shoulders—that's more like cat behavior."

"Maybe he was a cat in a previous life."

On her laptop, Ellen searched for the Quileute Oceanside Resort and called the number listed on their website.

Ellen explained her problem to the woman on the other end of the line and added, "I'm willing to pay ten thousand dollars for the week of Mother's Day if you can find me a house in La Push. Do you think there's a family who might want to give up their home for a week to make that kind of money?"

Sue lifted her brows.

"No," the woman said without hesitating, surprising Ellen. "The Quileute are private people. We're hospitable, yes, but no one would want to open their private home to strangers. I hope you can understand that."

"Of course," Ellen said. "But couldn't you ask around in case you're mistaken? There might be someone willing to do it for ten grand."

"I'll ask at our drum circle tomorrow night," the woman said. "But don't get your hopes up. Even if someone is willing, the tribal council will need to approve it."

"I'll donate an additional five thousand to the tribe," Ellen said.

Sue lifted her brows again. "This is getting to be an expensive birthday present."

Ellen covered the phone and whispered, "It's my fault, so I'm paying." Then, into the phone, she added, "Please?"

"I'll mention it," the woman conceded. "But some things are more sacred than money."

"I understand." Ellen worried she wouldn't be able to fix this after all. "Let me give you my name and phone number, just in case." After ending her call, she said to Sue, "I'll start phoning other places nearby. I know Tanya wanted La Push, but . . ."

"Like I said, I've called every single place within an hour's drive—even the sketchy motels."

"There's always Seattle."

Sue frowned.

"I know," Ellen admitted. "It wouldn't be the same."

"Not by a long shot. It's three hours from everything."

"You tried Port Angeles?" Ellen asked.

"Yep. Apparently, the Mother's Day week is the last week before all the rates double for the summer, and so everyone who can goes then."

"Oh."

Sue stood up. "When should we break the news to Tanya?"

"Let's give the Quileute tribe a chance to respond to my offer first, okay?" Ellen pulled Moseby into her arms and stood up, too.

Sue sighed and headed for the front door. "Let's not wait until the last minute to tell her. That would be cruel."

"We won't. I promise. I'm so sorry, Sue."

"Well, I forgive you. It's Tanya you have to worry about."

Sue gave her a hug, which brought Ellen to tears. It felt good to know that her friend wasn't going to hold a grudge. But Sue had been right about Tanya. Of the three of them, Tanya was the one who had trouble with grudges. Tanya was kind, loving, compassionate, and the first to volunteer to help anyone in need, but when crossed, she could be unforgiving.

The next morning, while Brian was in the shower and Ellen sat sipping a cup of coffee with Moseby perched on her shoulder, Ellen's cell phone rang. She almost didn't answer it, because she didn't recognize the number, but at the last second, she swiped the green circle.

"Hello?"

"Ellen McManius?" a woman on the other end inquired.

"Yes, this is she." Ellen hoped it wasn't a telemarketer.

"My name is Dorothy Blaine. I'm a member of the Quileute tribal council."

Ellen sat up, causing Moseby to slide down her back to be wedged between her and the chair. "Oh? Yes. Hello!"

Ellen was surprised to be hearing from someone from the tribe so soon. The drum circle wouldn't happen until later that evening.

"I'm reaching out to you because Victoria told me about your offer for the week of Mother's Day."

"Oh, good," Ellen said, feeling hopeful. "Can we work something out, then?"

"That depends on you. I have a possible solution, but you may not like it."

Ellen took a deep breath. "I'm all ears."

Two days later, Ellen flew with Moseby to Seattle, where she rented an SUV—a white Nissan Rogue—and drove in the dark and through the rain for three hours toward La Push. The last two hours were on winding roads that had Ellen gripping the steering wheel and clenching her teeth.

Moseby whined. He sat in a carrier strapped in the front passenger seat.

"I know, Moseby-Mo. It's been a long car ride, but I think we're nearly there."

Brian had business meetings in Portland all week, and Ellen hadn't wanted to board the dog, worried it would cause post-traumatic stress disorder. Plus, she needed him, since she was traveling without her friends, hoping to get everything ready to save Tanya's birthday.

It was so dark and rainy in La Push when she arrived that she nearly missed the turn into the Oceanside Resort Office. She pulled in, put the rental in park, found the totem pole Dorothy had described, and, clutching her hood beneath her chin, used the phone inside the totem to telephone security.

"I'll be right there," a man on the other end of the line assured her.

Moments later, a black truck approached, and a police officer rolled down his window to hand her a key.

"Are you staying there alone?" he asked as she stood in the rain beside his truck. "I thought there were three of you. My paperwork shows three signatures."

Ellen and her friends had been asked to sign, scan, and email liability waivers.

"The other two will be joining me in a couple of days."

The officer frowned. "Are you sure that's a good idea, staying there alone? Dorothy told you about the history of the place, didn't she?"

"I'll be fine." Ellen sounded more confident than she felt. "I just need directions."

"It's up there on the highest hill," he pointed out. "Just follow this road on up. You can't miss it."

"Thank you," Ellen said.

"Let us know if you decide to leave early," the officer added, handing her his card with his contact information. "The cell service is spotty out here, but you can always drive over to the totem and call me from here."

"Will do." Ellen read the card. "Thank you, Officer Hobucket."

The officer waited until Ellen had returned to the SUV before he drove off. She said a prayer as she followed him from the parking area and back onto the road in the opposite direction, heading toward the beach, until she came to a fork. The road to the right went downhill and the road to the left went up, so she went left.

"This has to be it," she said to Mo as they neared a bungalow surrounded by enormous western red cedar trees, the silhouettes of which were visible in her headlights.

She parked the Nissan Rogue and took Moseby from his carrier. With his leash attached to his collar, she walked him toward the front door. It was too dark to make out much about its features. An old porchlight illuminated the front door and wooden porch, but not much else. She couldn't even tell what color it was painted. Maybe gray?

As she waited for Mo to do his business, she turned her face toward the ocean, but it was too dark to see. She could hear it, though, gathering in great bursts against rocks that must not be too far below. A glance to the dark sky above revealed no moon, but an ocean of stars twinkled down at her, and she felt suddenly small and nervous.

"Come on, Moseby-Mo." She nudged her dog from the grass toward the front door. "Let's check out the inside."

Dorothy had warned her that it hadn't been cleaned in years, and the stale air that greeted her when Ellen opened the door did nothing to contradict that.

Moseby whined at the stoop.

"Inside," Ellen commanded as she blindly felt the wall for a switch.

Not finding one, she stepped further into the bungalow, making the leash taut between her and Mo, who'd remained on the threshold.

Ellen's hand swept across a cobweb, and she gasped with surprise at the unexpected texture. Shuddering and wiping her hand against her jeans, she continued to flail around for a light switch and finally found a floor lamp when she walked right into it.

She dropped the leash by accident to steady the lamp, and Moseby scurried away.

Ellen rushed outside into the rain. "Mo! Come back here!"

Mo stood at their rental car looking back at her without any intention of minding her call.

Fortunately, he didn't run off as she approached him and scooped him into her arms.

"Why are you shaking, boy?" she said in a soothing voice. "Are you cold? I've got you. It's okay."

She fumbled for her phone, which was somewhere at the bottom of the purse draped over her shoulder. Once she found it, she turned on the flashlight app and proceeded back toward the house.

When she reached the porch, the front door, which she'd left ajar, slammed shut in her face.

"The wind is really something out here," Ellen remarked as she reached for the knob.

Finding it locked again, she balanced Mo in one arm as she fiddled around her front jeans' pocket for the key. Once inside with Moseby, she closed the door behind her, deciding to have a look around before fetching her bags.

The entrance led straight into a living area with a big picture window on the back wall that probably looked out over the sea. There was a fireplace to her right—small and unimposing—with a dusty old couch and a rocking chair near the hearth and the floor lamp that Ellen had nearly destroyed between them. There was no television or radio or rug or coffee table, though there was a painting on the mantle. Its subject appeared to be the bungalow—Ellen wasn't sure. She moved closer with her flashlight to study it, but Mo squirmed from her arms, and, nearly dropping him, she bent over to let him go.

He ran to the front door, where he sat and whined.

"Moseby." She put her hands on her hips. "This is home for a while. You better get used to it."

A *clack* came from the open kitchen, just to the left of the living area. Ellen's first thought was that there was a critter, like a rat or a raccoon. But Moseby would have been all over it. Instead, he cowered and whined.

Dorothy had warned her that the bungalow was haunted. That's why it hadn't been lived in or rented out since the eighties. Dorothy had shared some of the paranormal occurrences that had been reported over the years—furniture rearranged, silverware thrown across the room, and, on one occasion, scratches. Ellen clutched the *gris gris* bag around her neck as she took a few strides toward the kitchen. She wore her tourmaline ring for added protection.

"I come in peace," she stated as she fumbled through her purse for her saltshaker. "I mean you no harm."

A kitchen drawer opened, and something shiny flipped through the air and past Ellen's cheek. With a thud, it hit the wooden front door. Ellen sucked in air and ran to the door, where a fork was stuck in the wood inches above Moseby.

Ellen swept her dog up into her arms and rushed from the house to the Nissan, where she climbed inside and locked the doors.

"We're sleeping in here tonight," Ellen panted.

Then she took out her saltshaker and, with a trembling hand, sprinkled salt on the dashboard.

It was too late to call anyone. She sent a text to Brian, letting him know she'd arrived safely. He would see it first thing in the morning. Then she sat in the vehicle holding Moseby. She stared at the porchlight, panting and trembling, for several minutes, afraid to close her eyes. Surely whatever had attacked them wouldn't follow her to the car?

As an extra precaution, she backed the Rogue further away from the house, closer to the bottom of the gravel driveway. She could still see the front door dimly lit by the porchlight. She stared in its direction for a long time before she finally fell asleep.

CHAPTER TWO

The Apparition

A high-pitched cry brought Ellen from her sleep. She squinted against the morning sun shining into her review mirror. Even with the sun out, it was drizzling, but strangely, the rain seemed to be falling up instead of down.

The cry came again. A seagull. It flew just above the bungalow and then vanished behind a towering cedar tree. Ellen started the car and pulled up to the house before cutting the engine and having a look.

She gazed at the bungalow, seeing it clearly for the first time. Painted a cheery yellow with gray trim, the house looked charming and inviting with its wrap-around porch, especially with the sweeping views of the ocean, which Ellen could see without leaving the SUV. She wondered if the attack from the night before had happened in a dream.

Moseby lay curled in her lap, sleeping. She reached for her phone only to find it dead.

With no phone and no watch, she used the position of the sun behind them to estimate that it was between seven and eight in the morning.

"Time to get up, Moseby-Mo," she cooed sweetly.

The little black dog kissed her chin as she opened the car door and clipped on his leash. She decided to avoid the house for now to check out their surroundings.

She gave Mo a moment to sniff the grass, and then she led him around the back of the house, where the hill dropped steeply toward the beach. The wind blew her hood from her head, exposing her ears to the cold.

For a Texan, fifty degrees in May was a treat. Glad for the insulated windbreaker Brian had loaned her, she smiled against the crazy, sideways rain and continued to soak in the view.

Oceanside Resort was far below her to the north. She could see over the condominiums to the beach in front of them. Known as First Beach, it curved around the resort in the shape of a crescent moon and ended just below the bungalow. More than two dozen wooden steps cut into the hillside led from the bungalow to the beach.

"Careful, Moseby," she warned as they descended through thick grass growing on the hillside.

When she reached the wet sand at the base of the steep hill, Ellen stood in awe.

Three huge stones lay on the sand like sleeping elephants. They'd been carved by wind and sea into sculptural works of art. Behind her, the hill she had descended was also solid rock, hovering at a height three times as tall as she. The rock had been worn by the tide crashing into it. She touched the smooth, wavy surface. In some places, the ridges were wide and flouncy, like a pleated skirt. In others, they were thinner and more uniform, like a ruffled potato chip. It was amazing to her how the sea had sculpted the stone over time.

Yes, that's what she had heard last night: the sea doing its work.

Moseby tugged at his leash. She turned from the hillside and the rising sun to gaze at the sandy beach and the endless waves lapping at it. Mo drank from a tidepool. Not sure that it was a good idea, she stooped over the pool and, to her surprise, saw a beautiful red-orange starfish—not with pointy legs but curved ones. It looked less like a star than a five-petaled flower clinging to the side of a rock.

"How beautiful," she whispered.

Three different shells moved in the still water. Moseby barked.

"Those are hermit crabs. Aren't they cool?"

He looked at her and tilted his head.

She noticed three more fat starfish clustered together at the bottom of a rock, along with a strange, green sea anemone. Too bad her phone was dead. She would have loved to snap a few photos.

"Come on. Let's explore the rest of the beach."

She led him north, toward the resort, where the condominiums and cabins were separated from the sandy beach by a graveyard of dinosaur bones.

They weren't really bones, but ancient trees torn by their roots and left here ages ago. The petrified trunks were at least eight feet in diameter and many more feet long. They were sculptural and beautiful, and they created a natural barrier between the ocean tides and the resort. They had the added benefit of being on a hill, blocking the view of the buildings, making visitors on the beach feel as if they were miles away from civilization.

Ellen led Mo past the dinosaur graveyard further north. The wind was even fiercer this close to the water, but at least the rain had stopped.

Beyond the wet sand and surf were two long and narrow islands with a thin cluster of fir trees that looked like fringe. Beyond the islands, a river surged from the east and into the sea.

Moseby pulled the leash taut and growled. Ellen glanced his way just in time to see a harbor seal slide from a nearby boulder into the waves.

"Moseby! You scared it off. It was just a seal, you silly."

Ellen watched the water, hoping to catch sight of the gray-spotted seal again. After a while, Mo tugged at the leash. He wanted to investigate the dinosaur bones.

Allowing him to lead the way, she studied the petrified logs more closely, amazed by their sheer size. She felt like a hobbit standing beside them.

The rain began to fall more heavily, drenching her hair before she could manage to get her hood back on. She supposed it was time to head back anyway—though she had enjoyed having the magnificent beach all to themselves.

"Come on, Moseby. Let's get you some drinking water back at the house."

They followed the beach past the dinosaur graveyard and toward the imposing hill she now realized she would have to climb. It had been easy going down. Going up would be a different story.

At least the sudden downpour had ended, and it was merely sprinkling again.

"Pull, Moseby." She laughed at herself as she panted and struggled up the first dozen steps.

She stopped short when her dog rushed to her feet and cowered beside her, yipping and whining.

At first, she worried he had a splinter in his paw, but as she stooped over him, the hair raised on the back of her neck. Mo grew silent. She held her breath as she looked up at the steps a few feet ahead of them.

He was transparent but bright with the sun behind him beaming through his body. Enough of him was defined for her to make out Native American features. His long hair lay across one shoulder in a single braid that was freakishly still, even in the strong winds. With a wide stance and arms crossed, he was an imposing form at least six feet in height. Standing above her on the hillside, he seemed even larger.

"I—I come in peace." Ellen lifted Mo into her trembling arms and held him close. "I mean no harm."

Slowly, the transparent man shook his head from one side to the other.

"I'm a friend," she insisted. Ellen teetered on the verge of running toward the beach. "I want only to help. I can help you to move on and find peace."

Again, he slowly shook his head from one side to the other as she gazed at him in disbelief.

"What holds you here?" she asked. "Who are you? Will you speak with me? I have instruments in the car, they can help . . ."

Her voice faltered when the apparition disappeared.

Ellen stood there for many seconds, blinking, wondering if she had really seen the apparition. If Moseby hadn't reacted so strongly to it, she might have been able to convince herself that she'd only imagined it. But there was no doubt that he had witnessed something, too.

"At least he didn't throw a fork at us," she whispered to Mo as she carried him up the incredibly steep steps.

When she reached the top, she put Mo down, clutched her knees, and struggled to catch her breath, thinking how fit she would be if she lived here.

Once she could breathe again, she returned to the car and grabbed her broom and one of her bags—the one with the cleaning supplies—before heading to the house. Cautiously, she unlocked and opened the front door. Moseby whined.

"You don't have to go in if you don't want to," she said, noticing the fork still stuck in the door. "Would you rather hang out in the car in your carrier?"

As if he understood her, he wagged his tail and pulled on his leash toward the car. She set her stuff down on the porch and followed him.

"I'll bring you some food and water," she assured him after she'd tucked him into his carrier.

Then she dumped more of her bags and instruments on the front porch, where they were protected from the light rain that had begun to fall again. Finding Mo's food and water bowls, she entered the house, pausing at the threshold.

"I come in peace," she said again. "I mean you no harm. I've come to tidy up the house, okay? I just need to get my dog some food and water first."

Carefully, she crossed into the kitchen, where the one drawer remained open. She slapped it shut, wishing she had duct tape, so she could tape it closed. Then, with food and water bowls full, she returned to the Nissan to get Moseby settled. She left his window cracked—it was too cold to leave all the windows down, but she wanted to hear him if he cried out for her.

"I'll leave the house door open," she told him as he lapped up his water. "Call me if you need me."

She reentered the bungalow, determined to clean the house, both physically and spiritually. After plugging her phone and charger into a kitchen outlet, she took a deep breath and glanced around the house, wishing the tribe hadn't forbidden her from hiring local help. They didn't want outsiders knowing about their enchanted bungalow, fearing it would sabotage their Oceanside Resort, which was a significant source of tribal income.

And no one in the tribe could be paid any amount of money to set foot inside these walls.

"Ellen," she said to herself. "It's all up to you. You got us in this mess, and now you'll have to get us out of it."

First, she opened all the windows that would open—this excluded the large picture window along the back wall. There were two bedrooms on the right side, or north side, of the house—one at the front and one at the back. The back bedroom had a panoramic view of the beach, and Ellen decided the birthday girl should get that room.

Both rooms had French doors leading out to the wrap-around porch. They also had double beds with bare mattresses that were covered in a thick layer of dust. After opening the windows, Ellen carried each mattress to the porch to beat off the dirt and to allow the mattresses to air out while she cleaned the house.

On the opposite side of the house near the kitchen, a flight of stairs led to the third bedroom—a loft in the attic that overlooked the entrance below. Being a loft, it wasn't very private and had only one window. The view of the sea from that single window was amazing, but, although the loft was spacious, this was the least desirable room. Ellen decided she and Moseby would take it.

In the loft were two twin beds, also with bare mattresses. Ellen lugged them each down the stairs, one at a time, and took them past the small table and chairs and through the back door off the kitchen to the porch to repeat the process she'd performed on the others. She did the same with the three couch cushions, which were even dustier than the beds. The dust flew into her throat and made her cough and hack, but she was determined to make this house perfect for Tanya.

There was a tiny white bathroom beneath the stairwell—the only one in the house. It was cute, with an old-fashioned clawfoot tub in the shortest part of the room resting on black and white checkerboard linoleum that continued into the kitchen and stopped at the end of the stairwell, where honey-oak floorboards carried through the rest of the house. Ellen rummaged through her bags for toilet paper, towels, and soap and quickly outfitted and used the facilities before finding her sage smudge stick, abalone bowl, and lighter.

After bathing herself in its smoke, she carried her smudge stick from room to room, repeating, "Evil spirits are not welcome here. Fly away, never to return. I command all negative energy to flee this place immediately. You cannot be here."

It was easier to make demands in the light of day; nevertheless, Ellen was on edge, expecting the spirit to attack her as it had the previous night.

Once she had cleansed each room, she put the stick in her abalone bowl on the small kitchen table and left it there to burn out while she got to work cleaning all the windows and dusting every surface before sweeping every floor. She went outside to breathe in some fresh air and to check on Mo every so often, and except for once when he needed to be let outside, she found him sleeping soundly in his carrier.

She still needed to clean the bathroom and the kitchen when she decided to take a break and get something to eat. Her back was killing her, and she was covered in dust. She was washing her face at the bathroom sink when a chill snaked down her spine. Glancing in the mirror above the sink, she watched with horror as the bathroom door, which she'd left ajar, swung wide open, hitting against the side of the stairwell. She jumped and held her breath.

"Hello?" she finally said.

When nothing more occurred, she turned off the water with shaky hands, dried her face, and left the bathroom, only to discover the kitchen drawer open and another shiny utensil flinging through the air.

She screamed and ran from the house. She hesitated just outside the door, wondering if she should leave with the mattresses and cushions on the porch, along with all her bags and equipment. She supposed the area, being so high up on the hill and isolated, was safe enough from thieves. As she stood there contemplating what to do, the front door slammed shut behind her.

"Fine!" she shouted into the damp air. "But I'm coming back, whether you like it or not!"

CHAPTER THREE

More Preparations

The only restaurant in La Push was a one-minute drive past the condos and cabins to the river at the far end of First Beach. Rustic and cute, the River's Edge sat on a hill near the mouth where the Quillayute River flowed into the sea.

With Moseby snug in the cloth pooch carrier, Ellen entered and asked the young woman who greeted her if it was okay to bring her dog inside.

"He's welcome as long as he's well-mannered," she said.

"He'll be good. I promise."

The young woman nodded and led her to a table next to the windows, from which Ellen could see two seals playing in the river.

She couldn't wait for Sue and Tanya to experience this, too.

Mo licked her cheek and looked out the window while she glanced over the menu. When the waitress came, Ellen decided on fish and chips.

"Garlic fries or regular?" the waitress asked.

"Oh, what do you recommend?"

"Garlic. Definitely the garlic."

"Okay then. I'll have that."

Ellen and Moseby watched the seals while she waited on her order. It felt good to sit down and relax in a safe space.

Taking out her phone, she was relieved to find she had a few bars. She also had missed calls from Brian and Sue. She decided to put off calling them until she had better news to report.

But just as her fish and chips arrived, Sue called. Ellen answered.

"How's it going?" Sue asked.

"Great. I'm eating fish and garlic fries at a restaurant overlooking the river, where seals are playing in plain view." Ellen stuck a fry in her mouth.

"How magical! But garlic fries? How are they?"

"Delicious. They came highly recommended by the waitress. I'm glad I took her advice."

"They want to make sure you aren't a vampire."

Ellen laughed. "Maybe so. I did see a sign that marked the treaty line and read *No vampires beyond this point.*"

"How funny. How's the house?"

Ellen took a deep breath.

"Ellen? You there?"

"It's challenging," Ellen admitted.

"What do you mean? Is it run down? Should we cancel our flights?"

"No. The house is charming. It's the haunting I'm having trouble with."

"What kind of trouble?"

Ellen sighed, wondering how much to divulge. "I feel a negative presence. And I saw an apparition on the hill behind the house. It was a man—Native American. He shook his head, like he didn't want me to enter."

"You saw an apparition?"

Ellen glanced around the restaurant, realizing she was being overheard. She lowered her voice, "Mmm-hmm. And the sage smudge stick isn't working."

"Did you try holy water?"

"Not yet."

"Well, give that a try. And don't forget to salt everything."

"Will do. I'll call you later, okay? My food's getting cold."

Not long after Ellen put away her phone, a stranger approached her table—a young man with dark eyes and shoulder-length black hair. He appeared to be in his early twenties.

"Excuse me, ma'am. I heard you say you saw an apparition."

Ellen blushed. "Yes, I did."

"Would you mind telling me about it? I could come back when you're finished eating."

"It's okay." Ellen motioned for him to have a seat at the table. "If you don't mind me eating and talking at the same time."

"Of course not. I'm the one intruding." The young man was tall and lean. "Your dog is cute. What's his name?"

"This is Moseby."

"I'm Ben."

"Ellen. Nice to meet you. Do you live here, or are you a tourist like me?"

"I live here. I've lived here my whole life."

"Then you're Quileute?" Ellen asked.

Ben nodded. "I've seen apparitions, too. Did you see it on the hill near the enchanted bungalow?"

Ellen widened her eyes. "Yes. Is that where you've seen it?"

"Yes. As a kid, my parents warned me not to go there. All the parents tell their kids that the house belongs to Duskiya, the kelp-haired child snatcher."

Ellen took a sip of her water and shook her head. "The apparition I saw had a long braid of normal-looking hair, not kelp."

"They say our ancestors still roam the beaches, protecting us from Duskiya," the young man disclosed. "But when your parents tell you not to explore a place, well, that's the first thing the kids want to do. Well, not all the kids, I guess. Just the curious ones."

"Like you?"

The young man nodded. "Have you seen anything inside the house? I've always wanted to check it out"

Ellen wasn't sure how much to tell him. "You've never been inside?"

He widened his eyes. "No. It's forbidden."

"I definitely sense a negative presence," she admitted. "What do you know about Duskiya?"

He shrugged. "Not much. Only that he likes to kidnap small children, cook them, and eat them."

"Do you know of any actual victims?" Ellen asked before she ate another fry.

"No. I think they're just stories. But I do believe there's something evil in that house. I was hoping you could tell me something new."

"Sorry. I only just arrived last night."

"Well, I'll let you finish your meal in peace. Thanks for talking to me."

"My pleasure."

"Bye, Moseby," he said to the dog as he turned to go.

After the young man had left, Ellen Googled Duskiya only to find an image of an old man with deep wrinkles in his face and green, unruly hair. He looked nothing like the apparition she'd seen on the hill behind the enchanted bungalow. Aside from the image, Ellen learned nothing more than what the young man had told her, so she finished her meal and then touched base with Brian while she waited on her bill.

From the restaurant, she drove twenty minutes into Forks to shop. A place called Forks Outfitters carried groceries as well as home décor, so she bought a birthday cake for Tanya, a few bottles of wine, breakfast and sandwich ingredients, and snacks. She also picked up some duct tape and found a gray slipcover and two gray and yellow throw pillows for the old sofa. Once she'd returned to the bungalow, she left Moseby in his carrier with his window cracked before cautiously entering alone with the shopping bags in her fists.

"I come in peace," she said at the threshold.

Carefully, she went to the kitchen and put away the groceries. Then she used some of the duct tape to tape the silverware drawer shut.

She returned the couch cushions to the couch and added the slip-cover and pillows, happy with the transformation. After that, she returned the mattresses to the bedrooms and covered them with fresh linens she'd brought from home.

She was leery about entering the bathroom after what had happened, but nothing strange occurred as she scrubbed it clean.

Next to the bathroom, on the shortest part of the stairwell, was a small door leading to storage beneath the stairs. Ellen opened it to find it full of cobwebs and dirt. She decided to leave it be, since she had so much to do as it was, and turned her attention to the kitchen, where she wiped down the white cabinets and black Formica countertops before sweeping and mopping the white and black, checkerboard linoleum floor. Next, she washed the cups, plates, and bowls that were in their dusty cabinets and dried them using a towel she'd brought from home before putting them away. As she glanced around the room, inspecting her work, she was shocked to discover that the silverware drawer was open, the duct tape hanging from it like useless wings.

She stood there for a moment scanning the kitchen and living areas. Something was in the house with her, but she couldn't sense much about it.

After pulling the fork out of the front door and finding a butter knife near it on the floor, she gathered the rest of the silverware from the drawer, wrapped it in a towel, and took it outside where she laid it at the base of a tall cedar tree. Then she rummaged through her bags on the front porch looking for the holy water and her large salt cannister.

Finding them, she re-entered the bungalow, ready for war.

She began by taking her spray bottle of holy water and squirting it, like air freshener, throughout each room. "Evil spirits, fly away, never to return. You aren't welcome here. All negative energy must leave this place."

After cleansing each room with her words and holy water, she took her large salt cannister and sprinkled salt in the corners of every room as she repeated her commands to the evil spirits.

While she was in the bathroom sprinkling the salt and saying her words, she saw the door fling itself wide open, as it had done earlier that day. Ellen froze, waiting to see what would happen next.

When nothing more happened, she held her breath and left the bathroom, repeating in the kitchen, "Negative energy, evil entities, I banish you from this house. You cannot be here. Leave, never to return!"

Relieved that the kitchen drawer was empty of its silverware, Ellen was about to exit the kitchen when she felt something touch the back of her neck. She froze, paralyzed, unable to breathe. The touch had been light, almost like hot air. Had she imagined it? After several seconds had passed, she was finally able to turn around and look behind her. Although she couldn't see anything, she felt something ominous sucking all the air from the room.

She ran from the kitchen to the living room, clutching the salt cannister and her *gris gris* bag.

"Who are you?" she demanded, her heart pounding in her chest. "Why are you here, and what do you want?"

She pulled out her phone and opened her spirit box app, but she didn't have enough service to use it. Returning it to her purse, she found her pendulum, and holding it up in the air, she asked, "Do you mean to harm me? If so, please make this pendulum swing in a circle for yes. If not, please make it swing back and forth for no."

In less than a second, the pendulum swung in a circle.

Ellen glanced at the front door, tempted to run for her life, but she held her ground and bit her lip. "Please let my friends and I stay here for one week. If I promise to leave you alone—to stop trying to banish you—and if I promise we'll leave in one week, will you let us be? Please make the pendulum move in a circle for yes. Make it move back and forth for no."

The pendulum hung without moving. Even if it had moved, how much could she trust the answer of a malevolent being? And why on earth would anyone want to stay in a house with it for a week? Was she crazy?

"Hello? Are you still here?"

The pendulum moved in a circle.

"Is your name Duskiya?"

The pendulum slowed to a near-stop.

"Is there something you want me to do in exchange for your cooperation?" she asked, all the while thinking how stupid she was. Only a desperate person would attempt to make a deal with a devil.

The pendulum quickly moved in a circle.

Ellen wished her spirit box app worked. The pendulum only allowed for yes and no answers. For real communication, she needed the spirit box or the Ouija Board, the latter which she was too afraid to use alone.

Then, getting an idea, she rummaged through one of her bags for her sketch book and pencil box.

Sitting at the kitchen table, she said, "Maybe you can show me what you want from me. I'll close my eyes, and you work through me to draw what you want."

She gently moved the pencil back and forth along the bottom of the page, waiting for the ghost, or demon, or whatever it was, to guide her. Keeping her eyes closed, she said again, "Show me what you want me to do."

A few minutes passed as Ellen continued to move her pencil across the page. She kept her eyes closed and began to rock, trying to put herself into a trance. When nothing seemed to be working, she opened her eyes in frustration but was shocked to discover that her pencil had created a scene on the page after all. She recognized First Beach with its elephantine stones, the graveyard of dinosaur bones, and the small islands fringed with sparse trees. But what was horrifying about the drawing was Oceanside Resort. The condos lay in ruins as billows of smoke rose from them into the sky.

Stammering, Ellen whispered, "You want me to burn down the resort?"

Of its own accord, her pendulum lifted from the couch in the living room, swung in a circular motion, and then fell back onto the cushions.

Ellen jumped to her feet and fled the house, closing the door behind her. She climbed into her car, backed to the end of the driveaway, and sat there, panting, for many minutes.

Moseby yipped, snapping her out of it.

"I agree. Let's get out of here."

CHAPTER FOUR

The Librarian

After eating supper at the restaurant, Ellen left the rental car in the parking lot and took Moseby for a walk along the river. The rain had stopped, and the wind wasn't as strong here as it had been on the hill and the beach. With the sun falling in the west over the Pacific Ocean, the temperature had chilled to the mid-forties.

She hadn't yet gone very far when she came to a sign on a wire barrier that read: *Quileute Burial Grounds. Trespassing Strictly Prohibited.*

From where she stood, Ellen saw a field of grass without any graves—at least none marked. Confused, she turned back, saying to Mo, "Sorry this wasn't a very long walk, boy."

Returning to her vehicle, Ellen passed a building with a sign that read *Quileute Resource Center and Library.* She tucked Mo into his cloth pooch carrier and went inside to have a look around.

The building reminded her of the portables at her kids' elementary and middle schools, having the same musty smell and creaky floorboards covered in thin, industrial carpeting. Rows of floor-to-ceiling, metal shelves took up most of the room. A long, wooden conference table with ten chairs stood between the entrance and the shelves, and over in the corner near the front of the building was a wide desk behind which sat an older woman with white hair and dark brown eyes and a fleshy mole on her right cheek. She stared curiously at Ellen.

"Hi." Ellen grinned nervously as she removed her hood. "I hope it's okay that I brought my dog inside. He's well-behaved."

"Can I help you with something?" The woman wasn't exactly unfriendly, but she didn't seem happy to see Ellen.

"I hope so." Ellen moved closer to the desk. "I'm staying at the bungalow on the big hill, and I was hoping to find out more about its history. Do you have any books on it that I can check out?"

"Only tribal members can check out books. You're welcome to peruse the shelves and read anything you find here."

Ellen sighed. "Okay. I'm looking for information on the house. Dorothy Blaine told me that it was built in the late 1800's, and . . ."

"The original house was torn down. The bungalow was built in the thirties."

"Oh," Ellen hesitated. "Do you know anything else about it?"

"I'm an elder tribal member. I know everything there is to know about it."

Ellen gave the older woman her friendliest smile. "Would you mind telling me what you know?"

"Are you a reporter? An author? We have protocols for that."

Ellen shook her head and waved a hand in the air. "No. Nothing like that. I'm a paranormal investigator."

The older woman arched a brow.

Ellen rarely referred to herself that way since she had never intended to become one. One thing had led to another, and she still considered herself somewhat of an amateur. She took a deep breath. "There's something evil in that house, and it attacked me and my dog. I want to learn everything I possibly can, so my friends and I can banish it."

"Then you'd better pull up a chair and have a seat." The woman motioned to one of the chairs sitting around the conference table. "Would you like a cup of tea? I was just about to pour another one for myself."

"That would be lovely." Ellen tried to keep the surprise from her voice.

"I'll be right back." The older woman left the room with her empty cup.

Ellen dragged a chair from the conference table to the desk and had a seat. She took the opportunity to glance around, studying some of the more interesting artifacts on shelves along the wall. Of the baskets and painted wood, a carving of a black and red-orange salmon stood out, its colors boldly contrasting everything else in the room.

"Salmon are very important to our people." The older woman returned carrying two teacups on saucers. She handed one to Ellen. "Do you take honey in yours?"

"No, thank you."

"I'm Mary, by the way."

"Ellen. Nice to meet you. And this is Moseby."

Moseby, curled in his carrier in her lap, opened his eyes without moving his head and then closed them again.

Mary returned to her seat behind the desk. "Where should I begin?"

Ellen took a sip of the hot, soothing tea. "You said the bungalow was built in the thirties?"

"Yes, in the late thirties, not long after our corporate charter was issued to us by the U.S. secretary of the interior. It was intended to be a house of honor for the chief and his family because it sits on the highest point at the center of village life with the best views of the sea."

"And what changed?"

"Nothing, at first. When the chief died in his sleep a week after moving in, we thought it was from natural causes. He was quite old, you see—nearly ninety. But when the second chief died there two months later, well, then we had a pattern."

"You believe those deaths were caused by something supernatural?"

"Yes, we do."

Ellen shuddered. "Has anyone else died there?"

"In the forties and fifties, the house was rented to a white man who lived there for almost twenty years before he died."

"In the house?" Ellen hoped the woman would say no.

But Mary nodded. "It was a stroke or a heart attack. He was in his early eighties, just a few years older than I am now, but we don't believe his death was supernatural."

Nevertheless, Ellen would not be sharing that information with Tanya. "So, you think the ghost only attacks the chiefs?"

"Or tribal members. It seems to tolerate outsiders."

"Except that it attacked me and my dog."

"I'm sorry about that. You aren't obligated to stay. We can issue a refund for the rest of the week."

Ellen shook her head. "I'm not ready to give up yet."

The librarian arched her brow again.

"Dorothy told me the bungalow was a tourist rental for a while and that visitors reported all kinds of strange occurrences."

"It's true. We built Oceanside Resort in the late seventies and included the bungalow as one of the rentals, but the stories being reported by guests weren't good for business, so we closed it in the mid-eighties."

"It's such a charming house and, as you said, it's on prime property. Maybe my friends and I can figure out the identity of the evil entity haunting it. Maybe it will repent and move on. We've had some success with that in the past. If not, maybe we can banish it."

"Oh, we already know who's haunting our enchanted bungalow," Mary said nonchalantly before taking another sip of her tea.

"You do? How? Who is it? Duskiya?"

Mary laughed. "Duskiya? No. That's a children's story. It's Dan Pullen."

"Pullen? Like, rhymes with Cullen?"

Mary laughed again. "I hadn't thought of that, but yes."

"Speaking of Cullen, how do you and your people feel about *Twilight*? I bet it's been good for business."

"We do like the extra money from the influx of tourists to the area, yes." Mary frowned.

"But?"

"Well, cultural theft isn't very nice."

"I don't understand."

"The author didn't just reinvent our origin story, but . . ."

"I doubt readers believe you are descended from wolves." Ellen chuckled nervously.

"Oh, but we are. Our creation story speaks of a great Transformer. That part is true. But there were no vampires involved, and we certainly don't change back."

"Oh." Ellen tried to hide her surprise.

"You people believe your god transformed Adam from dirt and Eve from his rib, but a transformation from wolves is too farfetched?"

"No, of course not. I just didn't know there was even a kernel of truth to the story in *Twilight*."

"The worst part though is the tattoo that appears on the bodies of the actors representing the Quileute. Our stories were appropriated in its design, and because it's on merchandise in shops all over the country, it's come to be associated with us. It's a false representation using appropriated culture to make millions of dollars for the movie producers, the merchandisers, the shops—everyone but us, and without our permission."

"Oh. I understand now."

Mo lifted his head and gave Ellen an "I want something" look.

"Just a few more minutes, Moseby-Mo," Ellen said to him. To Mary, she asked, "So, who was Dan Pullen?"

"A white settler who thought he had a claim to the best land in this area."

"What made him think that?" Ellen wondered.

"Homesteading practices at the time. Settlers laid claim to lands occupied by Quileute up and down the river. We were pushed back all the way to this beach. At one point, we and other native peoples occupied this whole area—including what is now Olympic National Park."

Ellen frowned. "I guess that happened to native peoples all over the country."

"There's no guesswork needed. It did. And later Pullen, who worked at the trading post and managed a fur company, submitted a claim for property at the very center of our village life." Mary took another sip of her tea.

As badly as Ellen felt for the displacement of Native Americans, she could also see the point of view of the settlers, who'd been encouraged to claim homesteads throughout the U.S. to help suppress the "Indian problem."

Mary continued, "The claims usually took two years to be granted, but Pullen built his home before the permit came. He even rented buildings out to other settlers and businesses, making money on land that wasn't his."

"I can't believe he got away with that." Ellen was trying to be nice and didn't know what else to say. She could certainly believe it. American history was filled with similar stories.

"The Indian agents tried to put a stop to it, but Pullen was determined. Even after President Grover Cleveland issued his order in 1889 certifying this area as our reservation, Pullen and his wife argued that they had a prior claim to it. Our people had been here for thousands of years, yet they believed they had a prior claim."

"Is it possible the Pullens had a legal claim, if not a historical one?" Ellen asked.

"He and his wife thought so, but instead of waiting for the courts to decide his fate, Pullen took it into his own hands."

"What do you mean?"

"In the last weeks of summer, our people traveled every year to Puyallup to pick hops and make extra money. They camped for six weeks and socialized with other tribes that went for the same reason. But in 1889, seven months after Grover Cleveland had made our land an official reservation, Pullen and two others set fire to our twenty-nine long houses and burned down the village."

"Did you say *burned?*" Ellen shivered, recalling her drawing.

"Yes. My people lost everything, including our prized canoes, fishing gear, tools, artwork, and ceremonial regalia, which was sacred to us."

"Oh, no. You lost your history."

"No," Mary said sharply. "He couldn't take that away from us."

"Of course not."

"But we did lose precious historical artifacts that had been handed down through the centuries."

Ellen leaned forward. "Were the perpetrators arrested?"

"Everyone knew who did it. We had witnesses. And although the Indian agent made implications, no formal charges were ever made."

Ellen was beginning to understand how Pullen stood out from the other settlers. "That's seriously f-ed up."

"Tell me about it. To add insult to injury, during the six weeks my people were gone and unaware of what had happened, Pullen sowed grass on the razed village and enclosed it with barbed wire, preventing my people from returning to the land."

"How awful for your ancestors."

"Awful doesn't even begin to describe it. We nearly became extinct. It's our greatest survival story to date. While the lawyers battled over land rights in the courts, our people were forced to live on the beach for almost ten years, where tidal waves and tsunamis and other severe weather constantly threatened them. Even today, this building and the school across the street, along with several reservation houses, are in a tsunami zone. We're trying to get to higher ground, but it hasn't been easy."

"I can't even imagine. It's been over a hundred years."

"Yeah. Tell me about it."

"Why didn't the Quileute tear down the barbed wire and fight for their land?"

"We aren't a violent people, and we didn't want to risk losing the rez."

Ellen sucked in her lips and nodded. The natives had had so much more to lose than the Pullens if the law had acted against them.

"So, what happened to Dan Pullen?" Ellen asked.

"He was finally evicted by a court of law in 1898—nine years after Grover Cleveland had declared this land our rez—and he moved to Seattle. His wife and kids moved to Alaska. Pullen died twelve years later."

"In Seattle?"

"I believe so."

"Then what makes you think his spirit returned here? In my experience, ghosts usually haunt the places where they died."

"They can also haunt places they felt a strong connection to while alive," Mary pointed out. "Besides, he's buried just over the river, on a prairie not far from here, next to his brother. His spirit didn't have far to go to return to his 'castle'—that's what it used to be called, 'the castle.'"

"But you said it was torn down."

"Not at first. It was used as a schoolhouse for twelve years without any problems. Then, everything changed. Within months of Pullen's death, strange things began to happen—school desks were rearranged, books and materials would go missing. Nothing too serious. But as the months wore on, the pranks became more sinister—like teachers being pushed down the stairs—and the school was closed by 1912."

Ellen shivered. She hadn't considered that the ghost might try to push her or one of her friends down the stairs. "Is that when the house was torn down?"

"No. It remained standing until the thirties. It wasn't an easy decision to tear it down. There's a reason they called it the castle. It was an enormous, two-story home with bay windows two stories high, resembling a tower. It was an architectural beauty. Some called it ostentatious, but no one wanted to destroy it. My people wanted to repurpose it."

"Do you have any photos of it, maybe in one of these books?" Ellen was curious to see the "architectural beauty."

"There's a painting of it in the bungalow on the mantle over the fire-place. The council believes it belongs on the property, though I'd rather we preserved it here in the library. I've come close to taking it myself, but I can't bring myself to break the ban on entering."

"When did your tribe decide on the ban?"

"In the eighties when we stopped renting the bungalow out to tourists. Before then, only cleaning and maintenance crews were allowed to enter."

"I could bring you the painting," Ellen said with a nervous smile.

Mary chuckled. "I'll keep that in mind."

"Well, even if you don't want me to get the painting for you, I will do everything in my power to banish Pullen. Knowing his name will help."

Mary laughed again. "I like you, Ellen, but don't be too sure of yourself. I'm not just an elder and a librarian. I'm also a shaman, descended from a long line of other shamans. Don't you think we've tried everything? We thought burning the house down might do it, but obviously that didn't work, either."

"Has anyone tried salting and burning Pullen's bones?"

Mary's eyes widened. "We can't just dig up someone's grave without the family's permission. And how do you suppose the family would answer such a request?"

Ellen blushed. "Of course. I just thought drastic times might call for drastic measures."

"The tribe can't risk losing its charter by doing anything reckless."

"Of course not."

Moseby began to whimper.

"I better get back and get him fed." Ellen placed her empty cup and saucer on the desk. "Thanks so much for the chat and the tea."

As Ellen stood, Mary asked, "Do you mind if I give you a little advice?"

"Not at all."

"My people have been battling the ghost of Dan Pullen for decades—okay, maybe not in recent decades, because we've taken a break. As you probably know, spiritual warfare is draining."

Ellen nodded.

"We are a very spiritual people. We believe our ancestors live here alongside us. I interact with my grandparents on an almost daily basis. Ghosts aren't anything new or unusual to us. The concept of heaven is a state of mind, not a place, in our culture. We are surrounded by ghosts."

"Understood."

"So please accept my words of caution. If a spiritual people with thousands of years of tradition and connections to this land have not yet been successful in banishing the evil that is Dan Pullen, don't be too sure that you and your friends will have any better luck, okay?"

The blood rushed to Ellen's cheeks. "Would you blame us for trying?"

"No, but please be careful. Remove anything sharp from the premises. Avoid using anything flammable—including candles. And maybe try to trick him into thinking you're his friend."

"That's good advice. Thank you, Mary."

"I'm happy to help. I hope you'll come by again before you leave La Push and give me an update."

"I will do that. I promise."

"Let me know if I can be of further help to you," Mary added as Ellen reached the door.

Ellen waved. "Thanks again."

It was dark and cold and rainy when Ellen left the library. She took Mo from his carrier, worried he might need to potty. Then they hurried back to her rental, which was parked in front of the restaurant.

Once inside the Nissan Rogue, Mo started whining again.

"Are you hungry and thirsty?" His food and water bowls were empty. "Let's get back to the house."

As she drove past Oceanside Resort toward the hill and the enchanted bungalow, Ellen reflected on what she had learned from the librarian. Had she made a mistake in inviting her best friends to come and stay there? What if they could do nothing to stop the malevolent being occupying that house?

CHAPTER FIVE

A Night to Remember

The rain was pouring down again when Ellen reached the top of the hill and parked the Rogue. She pulled the straps of her purse and the cloth pooch carrier over her neck and one shoulder, tucked Mo inside the carrier, grabbed his food and water bowls, and made a run for it. Once they were on the porch and out of the rain, she slipped the key from her jean pocket and opened the door.

"I come in peace," she said before stepping over the threshold.

The floor lamp and kitchen lights had been left on, thank goodness. She carried Mo to the kitchen, where she refilled his food and water bowls. Then she set him down on the checkered linoleum floor. She was relieved when he stayed to eat.

She dropped her purse and the key on the table, took off her jacket, folded it over the back of a chair, and grabbed a water bottle from the fridge. Then she sat at the table to keep a close eye on her dog while he finished his food. Just because the silverware was gone didn't mean the ghost couldn't use something else to attack them.

"Do you need to go potty?" she asked Mo once he had finished.

He wagged his tail as she put on his leash and walked him outside to the porch. It was cold without her jacket, and the rain was still pouring. She could hear the waves below crashing against the rocks. The black sky was filled with tiny lights and just a sliver of a moon.

She stood on the porch while Mo stepped into the grass beneath the overhang and peed. Then he jumped back onto the porch.

"Good boy!" she said, glad it hadn't been a hassle because of the rain.

As they returned to the door, it slammed shut in her face.

"This wind is crazy, isn't it, Moseby-Mo?"

Ellen tried the knob, but just like the last time, she found it locked.

Moseby whined while Ellen fiddled in her pocket, searching for the key.

"Oh, no! I left it on the table!"

They went around the side of the porch to the first set of French doors but found them locked. Next, they went to the back of the house to the second set of French doors—they were also locked. The kitchen door? Locked!

She banged on the kitchen door and hollered, "Let me in, you . . ." she stopped herself from calling an evil spirit a derogatory name. "Please?"

The door wouldn't budge.

Although she'd left the rental car unlocked, she hadn't planned to spend a second night in it, but what choice did she have? She could have called security if she'd had her cell phone and the card the officer had given her the night before. They were both in her purse in the bunga-low.

"Come on, Mo," she said, defeated. "It looks like we're sleeping in the car again."

She hadn't been sitting in the rental long when the rain stopped, and she got an idea.

She put Mo's leash back on and, together, they headed down the hill toward the resort office using the flashlight on her phone as their only source of light. It was only a half-mile walk, and although it was cold, it wasn't unbearably so—not for this Texan who had been sick of the heat. The wind lightened up once they got to the main road, where it started sprinkling again.

"Sorry, Moseby-Mo," Ellen said of the rain. "We're almost there."

They followed the road toward the resort office, which was closed, but she'd known that. She went straight for the totem where she picked up the phone and called security, explaining what had happened. Officer Hobucket arrived in his black truck within minutes and drove her and her dog back up the hill.

On the way, the officer asked, "Everything okay . . . with the house?"

Appearing to be in his mid- to late-forties, he wore a genuine look of concern on his face.

Ellen took a deep breath and sighed. "There's definitely something that doesn't want me there, but I'm determined not to let it defeat me."

He gave her a sideways glance. "Are you sure that's a good idea?"

"Yes, but I'm not the sharpest tool in the shed."

He laughed at her joke, which made her feel better.

"This is my only spare." Officer Hobucket parked behind the Rogue and handed the key over. "I'll wait here for you to bring it back."

She nodded as she opened the passenger's side door.

"I'd go with you," he explained. "Except I'm not supposed to set foot on the property."

"I understand," she said. "Come on, Moseby."

Together, they ran through the rain. She unlocked the front door and said, "I come in peace." Then she ran inside, grabbed the original key from the table, and rushed back out with Mo to return the officer's spare.

"Thanks again," she said. "I'm so sorry to have troubled you."

"No trouble at all. Feel free to call again if you need me. Good night, and good luck."

As she and Mo returned to the house to find the door locked again, she tried to comfort herself with the knowledge that the ghost had never killed an outsider.

"Everything's going to be okay," she reassured Mo as she unlocked the door and opened it. Then she said once again, "I come in peace. I mean you no harm."

She tucked the key in her pocket before unlocking all the doors as a precaution. Then, leaving the downstairs lights on, she found her overnight bag and, together with her purse and phone charger, ascended the stairs.

"Come on, Mo. Let's try to get some sleep."

After changing out of her wet clothes into a nightgown, she made a circle of salt around the first twin bed, where Mo was already curled up and waiting for her. Then she climbed beside him beneath the covers, and, after giving Brian a quick call to catch up and to say goodnight, she hung up and tried to go to sleep.

Even with no moonlight coming in through the window and with her bedside lamp turned off, there was enough light coming into the loft from downstairs to see by. Every few minutes, she opened her eyes to make sure that she and Mo were safe and alone.

At some point, she must have fallen asleep, because the next thing she knew, she was turning in the bed to face Mo, whom she felt beside her near her hip, but when she made the turn, careful not to hurt him, she had a fright.

Mo was not there.

She jumped to her feet, certain that something had been on the bed with her.

"Mo?" she whispered.

She noticed him curled on the other twin bed, sleeping soundly, her circle of salt broken where he had crossed it on the floor.

"Oh no, Moseby-Mo," she said beneath her breath through trembling lips. "Oh, no."

Her dog had broken the circle and had allowed the ghost in. Had it been lying beside her on the bed? Had it been nestled against her hip?

She shivered as vomit rose to her throat. She forced it back down and, grabbing the cannister of salt from the nightstand, moved to the other bed where Mo was sleeping. As she made a new circle, she recited words Sue had taught her years ago—words that fell from her lips from memory:

Guardians of the North, South, East, and West,

Elements of Earth, Air, Fire, and Water,

Bless this circle and protect those within,

Whether father, mother, son, or daughter.

No unwanted entities shall enter,

And safety shall prevail in the center.

This circle is cast.

Grant it shall last.

Heeding the librarian's warning about avoiding all things flammable, Ellen did not light a candle for the most northern point on the circle, which would have reinforced its power. Instead, she placed her spray bottle of holy water there, on the nightstand, and prayed for protection as she climbed in bed beside Mo.

Better yet, she took the bottle and sprayed some water over the bed, allowing it to fall on her and Moseby and the bed coverings. Then she replaced the bottle and continued her prayers.

Many minutes, perhaps an hour, passed before she began to doze off again. No sooner had she drifted to sleep when a loud ruckus from downstairs woke her. She sat upright in the bed and froze, listening.

The house creaked in the wind. The waves crashed against the rocks below. But what was the clattering sound that had brought her from sleep? Had she dreamt it?

Hearing nothing more, she returned her head to the pillow, stroked Mo's fur, and tried again to go to sleep. Within moments, she heard the sound again. This time, the *clackety-clack* was clear as day. She gasped, sat up again, and listened.

Moseby sat up, too.

"Hello?" she called from her bed.

There was another *clackety-clack, clackety-clack.*

Ellen agonized over what to do. Should she leave the protection of her circle to investigate? Or should she ignore what was most likely the taunting of a ghost, intent on luring her downstairs?

Her heart was beating so hard and fast that she could hear it, and it competed with the tapping sounds downstairs.

"Mo, what should we do?" she whispered.

Although she'd expected no answer, he jumped from the bed and raced down the stairs before she could stop him.

"Mo! Wait!"

She climbed from the bed and followed.

When she reached the foot of the stairs, her heart stopped. The window over the kitchen sink was open just a crack and slipping into the house through the opening were the pieces of the silverware she had removed from the house and put beneath a tree. The *clackety-clack* was the sound of each piece falling into the sink below the window.

Ellen covered her mouth and screamed into her hand. In the next moment, all the doors to the kitchen cabinets flung open, as did every drawer. Then silverware rose from the bottom of the sink and whipped through the air in her direction. She screamed again and ran out of the way, into the living room, as the pieces clattered to the floor by the stairs. Moseby scratched at the front door, whining.

Before Ellen could think of what to do, the front door opened, and Mo ran out.

"Moseby, wait!" She ran after him into the cold and rainy night.

Mo waited by the Rogue. As she hurried toward him in her bare feet, she slipped and fell in the mud on her hands and knees, the small rocks biting into her skin and probably breaking it. With sore hands and knee-caps, she attempted to climb to her feet but slipped again and fell on her backside.

The second fall hadn't hurt as much as the first, yet it was enough to make her cry. She was tired, frightened, cold, and covered in mud, and she'd had just about enough. She loved Tanya, but maybe it was time to call it quits. Maybe it was time to cancel the birthday trip and get the hell out of there.

Mo came to her side and licked her tears.

"Thank you, boy," she said. "I'm so sorry that I've put you through this for nothing. I give up, okay, boy? I give up. We'll sleep in the car and leave in the morning."

But once she climbed to her feet and saw how muddy she was, she knew she couldn't get into the rental in this condition. She'd need to change into clean clothes first.

She considered taking off the gown and sleeping nude. Who would see her anyway? But she just couldn't bring herself to do it. She'd rather face the ghost again than be seen naked by a passerby. Besides, the mud covered her arms and legs, and there was little hope of her getting it all off, even in the rain.

Bent over, holding Mo by the collar so as not to get him muddy, too, she led him to the porch to the front door which, she should have known, was locked.

She kicked the door as more tears fell from her eyes and sobs shook her body.

"You win!" she hollered. "Let me in so I can get my things, and I'll leave! You win!"

To her surprise, the front door opened.

Still holding Mo by the collar, she led him inside and closed the door behind them. She stripped out of the muddy gown and hung it on the doorknob, so as not to get mud everywhere. Then she crept in her bare feet past the silverware strewn on the floor to rinse off in the tub. Mo followed her.

Upstairs, Mo hopped onto one of the beds while she dressed and packed some of her things. She'd leave the bedding and the toiletries and the cleaning supplies and the groceries and just take her instruments and clothes—except for the muddy gown. It and everything else she'd leave behind was replaceable.

She unplugged her charger and carried her stuff downstairs. She was so tired, too tired to pack the car. It would have to wait until morning. She put her bags on the porch and carried Mo out to the car with her.

"Let's get a few more hours sleep," she said to him.

She kissed the top of his head and then tucked him into his plastic carrier, which was still strapped to the passenger's seat.

She supposed it was good that she'd tried to sleep in the house instead of waiting until her friends had arrived. It was better for Tanya if Ellen admitted the truth now than if Tanya had come and had been attacked without warning. Ellen doubted her friend would have been able to forgive her—not for a very long time, anyway. As much as Tanya would be disappointed over a canceled birthday trip, an attack by a malevolent being—one that Ellen knew about—would have been far worse.

Ellen would call her friends first thing in the morning to tell them to cancel their flights.

The ringing of her cell phone awakened Ellen. It was Sue calling at five in the morning. The sun hadn't yet begun to rise, but the eastern horizon was striped with a dim, predawn light.

"Why are you calling me so early?" Ellen yawned by way of a greeting.

"Oh, I forgot about the time difference. It's seven here, you know."

"That's still too early for a phone call. Is everything okay?"

"Everything's great," Sue said. "I just wanted to warn you that we'll be arriving earlier than planned."

"Wait. What?"

"Our flight was overbooked, so the airline called me and offered us earlier flights at a discount."

"Since when do you care about discounts?"

"Since never, but you know Tanya. She's over the moon about it. And now you don't have to wait up until midnight for us. Isn't that better? The earlier flight was the one we wanted in the first place, when you and I were planning this trip, but they didn't have three seats. Remember? Anyway, we arrive in Seattle at ten a.m. your time and should make it to La Push by two or two-thirty this afternoon. We're going to lunch in Seattle before the drive because ten o'clock will be like noon to us."

Ellen sat up in her seat. "Sue, I was going to call you and tell you to cancel your flights."

"What? We've already boarded the plane."

Ellen heard Tanya beside her ask, "What's wrong?"

"Everything okay, Ellen?" Sue asked.

Ellen fell back in her seat and took a long, deep breath.

"Ellen?" Tanya said into the phone. "What's wrong? And if you're messing with me, I'll strangle you."

"Nothing's wrong, birthday girl! I was just kidding. Everything's fine. I can't wait for you to get here."

"We can't wait, either!" Tanya cried.

"Awesome. Put Sue back on. Will you?"

"Ellen?" Sue asked.

"Everything's fine," Ellen said with forced cheeriness. "Call me when you're close."

"La Push, baby!" Tanya hollered into the phone. "Best birthday ever!"

"See you soon, Ellen," Sue said. "I have to hang up now for take-off."

After the call, Ellen sat in the Rogue watching the sunrise and wondering what the heck she was going to do. There was really only one answer to that question—at least only one she could think of.

She took Mo from his carrier and walked him to the back of the house. It wasn't raining, and the rising sun held the promise of a beautiful day. She gazed out at the sea and prayed to the heavens to forgive her for what she was about to do.

Ellen entered the house through the kitchen door, and, with Mo in her arms, she said, "I'll do it, Dan Pullen. For one week of peace in this house, in exchange for safety for me and my two friends and my dog, I promise to burn Oceanside Resort to the ground after the week is up. Do we have a deal?"

As if in answer, the silverware that had been strewn on the floor lifted into the air and slowly floated back to their drawer. Ellen held her breath and watched with wide eyes as the cabinet doors, which had been left open, closed. All the drawers closed, too. The window over the sink shut, and the pendulum, which she'd left on the couch, lifted into the air, swung in a circle, and fell to the couch again.

Mo whined in Ellen's trembling arms.

She didn't blame him. She'd just made a deal with the devil and, although she had no intention of going through with her side of the bargain, she was terrified that the ghost of Dan Pullen would sense her intentions before she could do anything about it.

CHAPTER SIX

The Birthday Girl

It was two-thirty when Ellen heard a car coming up the gravel drive to the enchanted bungalow. She had just finished eating a cheese sandwich at the kitchen table. She swept a few crumbs from the table onto her paper plate, laid it in the garbage bin, and rushed outside to meet her friends, leaving Mo where he'd been curled on the couch.

Ever since she had struck her bargain with the malevolent being sharing her bungalow, she and Mo had been left in peace. However, her anxiety returned with the arrival of her friends, and she hoped and prayed the ghost wouldn't terrorize them into submission, too.

"This is incredible!" Tanya cried as she stepped from the passenger side of the black Chevy Traverse Sue had rented in Seattle. Tanya's long, blonde hair danced like fire in the strong wind. "I've never seen such amazing views!"

"Happy Birthday!" Ellen smiled as she gave her tall, lean friend a hug.

"Thank you!" Tanya said. "What happened to your hand?"

Ellen hid her hands in her jacket pocket. "Oh, I fell. But it's fine. A little scrape is all. How was the flight?"

"Not bad." Sue stepped out from behind the Traverse. "And the drive was beautiful."

"I wouldn't know," Ellen said with a laugh. "It was dark and raining when I made it."

"Well, show us the house," Tanya urged. "It's adorable on the outside. Love the porch."

"Yes, it's charming," Sue agreed.

"The porch wraps all the way around." Ellen led them to the door, realizing for the first time that she should have bought some patio furniture. "And your bedrooms have French doors that open out to it. Come and see."

Ellen said another little prayer that the ghost of Dan Pullen would keep his side of their bargain as she led her friends into the house and showed them around. Moseby greeted them and skipped around the house after them, excited for visitors. He danced in front of Tanya.

"He wants to go between your legs," Sue explained. Then turning to Ellen, Sue said, "Tanya won't mind. She'll open her legs for anyone."

The three friends laughed as Moseby ran between Tanya's feet and then did the same with Sue.

"I'm glad we got that over with," Sue said. "Now we can continue with the tour."

Tanya opened the French doors leading from what was to be her bedroom. "I just can't get over these views. Makes me want to live here."

"Well, just wait for the rain," Ellen pointed out. "Otherwise, yes, it's lovely here."

Sue pulled Ellen aside and whispered, "I thought you were getting a cake and flowers."

"The cake is on the kitchen countertop. I forgot the flowers. This place was a mess, Sue. I worked my tail off getting it cleaned up. Cut me some slack."

"Did you get sixty candles?"

Ellen lifted her brows. "No. And we aren't supposed to light any candles anyway."

"Why not?"

"What are you two whispering about over there?" Tanya questioned as she re-entered her room from the porch.

"Just birthday surprise stuff," Ellen fibbed. "Why don't you take a walk on the beach while I help Sue with the luggage?"

"I saw you brought equipment," Tanya noted of the paranormal investigation equipment they had passed in the living room.

"I'm sure it's just for fun, if we want to," Sue said nonchalantly as she headed back into the main room. "This place does have a lot of history, after all."

"I doubt we'll have time for it though," Ellen added, following. "Come on, I'll show you the path down to the beach."

Ellen put Mo on his leash and led them through the back door to the steep steps overlooking the shore below.

"It's a little harder coming up than going down," Ellen warned. "Go have a look, Tanya. Sue and I will get the luggage."

"We aren't going to wait on her hand and foot for the entire trip, are we?" Sue asked within earshot of Tanya. "If so, I think I'll head home now."

Ellen and Tanya laughed.

"I can get my own suitcase," Tanya said.

"I got it," Ellen said. "Go check out the beach. It's breathtaking."

As Tanya descended the steps, Ellen and Sue returned to the Chevy Traverse with Moseby.

"Now tell me the truth," Sue pressed. "Why did you want us to cancel our flights?"

Ellen sucked in her lips, unsure of how much to divulge. "It hasn't been easy. The house is haunted by a man who tried to steal this property from the Quileute. I talked with a tribal elder—a librarian—last night."

"Did the holy water get rid of him?"

"For the time being," Ellen lied as she opened the hatch and grabbed Tanya's suitcase. "But I'm not sure how long it will hold him off. He's been haunting this area since his death in 1910."

"Better not mention this to Tanya."

"No. I agree. And let's avoid conducting any investigations in case it draws him back."

"Good idea." Sue dragged her suitcase behind her as she followed Ellen back to the house.

Ellen showed Sue to her room.

"It really is a great house." Sue opened the French doors from her room and gazed at the sea, her brown hair swirling around her head from the wind. "Where are you sleeping?"

"There's a loft upstairs."

"Is it nice up there?"

"Yeah. It's great. Perfect for Moseby and me."

"I'll take your word for it. I don't want to climb anything I don't have to. Tanya's got me nervous about tomorrow's plans."

"You mean hiking in the rain forest?" Ellen asked.

"Yeah. Apparently, you have to work hard to see the views of the falls."

"All the reviews I've read say it's so worth it, Sue."

"Well, I'm not everyone. I wouldn't mind making a pitcher of margaritas and sitting out here on the porch enjoying the views we've already got."

"I should have bought patio furniture."

"Why don't I do that while you and Tanya take a walk this afternoon? I want to pick out the chairs, anyway."

"Sounds great. Mo and I will go meet up with her now."

"I'll get flowers and candles, too. Maybe stuff for margaritas?"

"I bought wine."

"It's nice to have a variety."

"Don't get candles. Fire provokes the ghost."

Sue lifted her brows. "You know this from experience?"

"Yes. And it's a long story. We'll talk more later."

Ellen followed Moseby down the steep steps in the side of the hill to the beach below. The tide was high, leaving less sandy beach than had been there in the morning. Ellen was sorry that Tanya had missed the tide pools filled with starfish and other beautiful creatures and made a mental note to take her for another walk tomorrow after sunrise.

As she rounded the corner toward the dinosaur graveyard, Ellen caught her breath. Standing near one of the petrified logs talking with Tanya and pointing to the bungalow on the hill was Ben, the young man who had been curious about Ellen's apparition sighting. Ellen's stomach tightened as she rushed over, waving to them, trying to distract Ben from saying too much. Had he told Tanya the secret of the bungalow?

"Hey!" Ellen said, panting, as she caught up to them. "I see you met Ben."

"I was just telling her the stories about Duskiya," the young man said.

"Great." Ellen forced a smile as Tanya gave her a suspicious look. "The librarian told me they're only stories."

"Then why are tribal members forbidden from entering the bungalow?" Tanya wanted to know.

"Oh, superstitions and such," Ellen said dismissively.

Ben frowned, and Ellen felt a wave of guilt for belittling his people in front of him just to save face with Tanya.

"You said you saw an apparition," Ben pointed out. "Was *that* a superstition?"

"You saw an apparition?" Tanya asked Ellen accusingly.

"Well, yes, but you see," Ellen took a deep breath, "Mary—the librarian and a tribal elder—told me that Quileute ancestors dwell here among the living. It was probably her grandfather or some other relative. Nothing to worry about, Tanya."

"Why do I get the feeling you're not telling me something?" Tanya wanted to know.

"Because you're paranoid?" Ellen forced a laugh and added, "Come on. Maybe we can sight a harbor seal."

"Oh, you will," Ben said. "They're usually pretty active right now over by the river mouth."

"What about orcas?" Tanya asked him.

"Maybe from the top of the hill, near the enchanted bungalow," Ben said.

"Enchanted?" Tanya repeated.

"That's what we call it," Ben explained as he continued in the opposite direction.

As she passed him, Ellen whispered to Ben, "Sorry I said your people are superstitious. I just don't want my friend to worry."

Ben smiled. "I get it. Enjoy your walk."

Ellen and Tanya continued past the giant, petrified cedar trees toward the mouth of the river.

"According to my research," Tanya began, "those islands are called James Island and Little James."

"Oh, really?" Ellen was grateful for the change in subject.

"When a chief passed away, the Quileute people used to lay them to rest in canoes that they then perched in the tops of those trees on James Island. They can trace this practice back as far as seven thousand years ago."

"Wow," Ellen breathed. "No wonder this area is so important to them."

"What do you mean?"

Ellen told Tanya what she had learned about Dan Pullen from the librarian—omitting the parts about his ghost haunting the area and terrorizing Ellen into making an impossible deal with him.

"How sad," Tanya said when Ellen had finished.

"It really is. They're still trying to get out of the tsunami zone."

Tanya's eyes widened. "Are we in a tsunami zone?"

"Not where we are. No, it's over by the river."

"Are you sure?"

"Oh, look!" Ellen pointed to a group of three harbor seals swimming toward them from James Island.

"They're so cute!" Tanya cried.

Moseby barked excitedly.

"That's enough, Moseby-Mo," Ellen scolded. "No barking. Those seals are our friends."

"How incredible," Tanya said. "This place is amazing."

"It really is."

"I read that the name La Push comes from the French word *la bouche*, or mouth, because of the river mouth."

"That's interesting," Ellen said.

As they stood watching the seals playing in the sea, Tanya said, "I can't thank you and Sue enough for planning this trip for me. I think this is the most beautiful place I've ever visited."

Just then, it began to rain.

Tanya looked up and laughed. "I really don't mind the rain. It's so much better than the heat."

"Cheers to that!" Ellen said with a laugh.

They watched the seals for a few more minutes and then headed back toward the bungalow, passing Ben as he walked in the opposite direction.

"It's strange that his people are forbidden from entering the house," Tanya considered. "How can they rent it out if they can't get in there to maintain it?"

"I guess they hire outsiders to manage the property for them."

"I guess so. Still, I wonder why they won't go inside."

Tanya studied Ellen, and Ellen felt the blood race to her cheeks as she shrugged and pretended that she had no idea.

An hour later, Sue returned from Forks with three sturdy, stackable, outdoor chairs made of black iron and thickly woven, coated wicker.

"These must have cost you a pretty penny," Tanya said as she grabbed one from the back of the Traverse. "How will we get them back on the plane?"

"I'll just donate them to the tribe," Sue said waiting for Ellen to hand her one. "What's the use of having these gorgeous views if we can't sit out on the porch and enjoy them in comfort?"

"I'm surprised the property didn't come with them," Tanya stated. "You would think it would be a selling point to renting this place out."

"You would think," Ellen repeated as she took the third chair from the vehicle and headed toward the house.

"I bought firewood, too," Sue continued. "It's on the floorboard behind the passenger's seat, if one of you wouldn't mind grabbing it for me."

Ellen closed her eyes and sighed as she reached the porch.

"You okay, Ellen?" Tanya asked.

"This is heavy," she groaned with a laugh as she hauled the chair to the back of the house, her friends not far behind her.

"They are heavy," Tanya agreed, setting her chair down beside Ellen's.

"I didn't want to risk buying something that I could fall through," Sue explained.

Ellen shook her head. "Well, it would take an elephant to fall through these."

The three friends returned to the Traverse for another load. Ellen grabbed the firewood, Tanya the flowers, and Sue the margarita supplies before returning inside, where Moseby was waiting for them.

As Ellen laid the firewood in a pile beside the hearth, an uneasy feeling swept over her, as if the spirit of Dan Pullen were rejoicing over the prospect of a fire.

<u>CHAPTER SEVEN</u>

A Slip of the Tongue

The next morning, Ellen awoke refreshed from a perfectly enjoyable evening. They'd had margaritas on the porch at sunset, dinner at River's Edge Restaurant with the seals in full sight, and cake and wine before a cozy fire, where they had stayed past midnight. Now, Ellen woke to the smell of coffee, relieved that the night had been free of ghostly trauma. She changed clothes, put on her boots, grabbed her phone, and led Mo downstairs where she found Sue in the kitchen at the table with a breakfast of birthday cake and coffee.

"Happy Mother's Day," Ellen said to her.

"Happy Mother's Day. I'm shocked that both my kids have already texted me this morning."

"Well, they are two hours ahead of us," Ellen reminded her.

"Don't burst my bubble." Sue took a sip of her coffee.

"How did you sleep?" Ellen asked as she poured herself a half a cup.

"Horribly. I had a dream that a ghost set my bed on fire. I kept waking up all night, expecting to find myself in flames."

Ellen froze, worried that Dan Pullen had been the cause.

Tanya, whom Ellen hadn't seen lying down on the couch, sat up. "I hope it wasn't prophetic! Geez!"

Then Sue said, "If my dreams were prophetic, I'd be married to Leonardo DiCaprio. I don't think we have anything to worry about."

Ellen and Tanya laughed.

"Happy Mother's Day," Tanya said to Ellen.

"Same to you, birthday girl. How did you sleep last night? Your bed okay?"

"I slept like a baby," Tanya cooed. "For most of the night, I thought I was in my own bed with Dave snuggled up against me."

A chill ran down Ellen's spine as she recalled the sensation of Moseby lying beside her the night before when he hadn't been there at all.

"I need to take Mo for his morning walk. Anyone care to join me? The tide will be low, and we're bound to see starfish in the tidepools."

"I think I'll get enough walking in the rain forest," Sue said. "That's a hard pass for me. I'm gonna have my cake and eat it, too. But I'd love it if you took some photos of the starfish."

"What about you, Tanya?"

"I'll catch up with you as soon as I finish this cup of coffee," Tanya said to Ellen.

As Ellen headed out the back door with Mo, she whispered to the ghost, "Remember our deal."

Two hours later, Ellen, Moseby, and her friends had just completed a one-mile hike of the Spruces Nature Trail in the Hoh Rain Forest and were about to begin a shorter trail called the Hall of Mosses.

The trees towered over them with moss draping from the branches like long curtains in a variety of greens—olive, fluorescent, emerald, teal, and sea foam. The overhead canopy allowed plenty of dappled sunlight to trickle down, making gorgeous photo opportunities. Because she didn't like to be in photos, Sue had insisted on taking them of Ellen and Tanya—and sometimes Moseby—posing before a curtain of moss, or in a nook beneath a tree resembling a hobbit hole. The frequent breaks for photo-taking, along with the relatively flat slope of the trails, had made the hike pleasant for them—Sue included.

And Ellen hadn't seen Moseby this enthusiastic since she and Brian had adopted him.

But later, after lunching at a hamburger stand called the Hard Rain Café, they drove up to Lake Crescent to hike another part of Olympic National Park to see Marymere and Sol Duc Falls. The hikes in that region were more strenuous, and more than once Ellen and Sue told Tanya to go on without them. They were still able to enjoy views of the falls, just not from the highest vantage points.

They captured lots of great photos. Ellen forced Sue to get in some of them, too. Once, the four of them posed together as a passerby took the photo with Sue's phone.

"Thank you," Sue said to the man as she retrieved her phone. Then to her friends, she muttered, "I'll be sure to delete that one. I look horrible."

"Give it to me." Tanya took the phone. "You do not look horrible. You look great. Do not delete it. We don't have many photos together, and I want to remember us on my birthday trip."

Sue sighed. "I should have known you'd play the birthday card."

"I'm so glad y'all were able to get an earlier flight," Ellen said, changing the subject. "I doubt we would have started off the day as early as we did if you had arrived after midnight."

"I know we wouldn't have," Tanya agreed. "I needed a second cup of coffee as it was."

"That was because of the margaritas," Sue said.

"And probably the wine," Ellen added.

"I guess it's a good thing you dropped the ball, after all," Sue said to Ellen.

Ellen blanched, wondering what Sue had been thinking to mention her mistake in front of Tanya.

"Dropped what ball?" Tanya wanted to know.

Sue quickly realized her mistake as she pointed into the forest and cried, "What is that? Is that an elk?"

Sure enough, it *was* an elk. It was bigger than the Chevy Traverse and only twenty feet away from them. Sue quickly snapped a photo.

Ellen was surprised that Moseby wasn't barking at the enormous animal. Instead, he was busy sniffing a clump of grass.

"How incredible," Tanya whispered. "I've never seen one so big and so close up."

Ellen could think of only one thing: the gratitude she felt toward the elk for distracting Tanya from Sue's slip of the tongue.

As they were heading back to their vehicles, Tanya mused, "With all the water that we've been drinking, I'm surprised we haven't had to pee."

"I think when the body is focused on breathing and pumping blood," Ellen said, still panting, "the bladder takes a back seat."

"Or maybe your therapy is paying off," Sue said to Tanya. Turning to Ellen, she added, "It turns out her bladder isn't the size of a pea after all."

Ellen glanced at Tanya, who explained, "My doctor prescribed pelvic therapy to control my frequent urination. You should look into it, too, Ellen. It seems to be working."

Sue stopped to catch her breath. "Too bad the therapist is a woman and not an attractive man our age—or a tiny bit younger."

"Why would you say that?" Ellen wrinkled her nose at Sue.

"Tanya?" Sue prompted. "Care to share the details?"

Tanya lowered her voice. "I didn't realize the therapist was going to stick her finger up in me and tell me to squeeze as hard as I could. It caught me off guard, but she said I did well."

Ellen giggled at how proud Tanya seemed to be of her Kegel strength.

"Did it feel good?" Ellen teased.

Tanya rolled her eyes. "Oh, stop. You sound like Sue."

"If the therapist had been an attractive man our age—or a tiny bit younger—I bet it would have," Sue taunted as she continued walking toward the parking lot.

Ellen busted out laughing. "And Tanya might have been able to squeeze even harder!"

"Did you ever tell Dave?" Sue asked. "I bet he would have liked to watch."

Tanya chuckled. "Well, maybe so. He does want me to have a sister wife. He's been watching that Netflix show about the polygamists and keeps hinting that we could give it a try."

"Does he have someone in mind?" Sue asked.

"It would be you, of course, if you weren't already married to Tom," Tanya teased.

Ellen made a face of mock reproach. "I'm jealous. I want to be sister wives."

"If only we could be sister wives without the husbands," Tanya said with a giggle.

"I think that's called lesbianism," Sue stated as they reached the car.

"Sister wives without the sex, I mean," Tanya added.

A couple who'd been getting out of the car next to the Traverse looked at them curiously. Ellen felt the blood rush to her cheeks as embarrassment swept over her. Sue giggled as she climbed behind the wheel. Ellen helped Mo into the back seat with her.

"I'm glad we returned the Rogue instead of this Traverse," Ellen said. "I think the back seat is roomier. Don't you?"

"I think the Rogue is better looking," Sue insisted, "but if comfort is your thing, then we made the right decision."

"Like comfort isn't your thing," Ellen teased.

Tanya chuckled. "I think she just has a thing for rogues."

"Too bad Tom isn't one," Sue said as she buckled her seatbelt. "Anyway, I've been known to suffer for the sake of good looks. All of this," she waved a hand across her face and body, "doesn't happen without a little discomfort."

Tanya and Ellen laughed.

"So, Ellen?" Tanya asked from the passenger's seat. "What ball did you drop?"

Well, heck, Ellen thought. She glanced at Sue's reflection in the rearview mirror, hoping for help. When none came, Ellen said, "I was supposed to make dinner reservations at Bella Italia in Port Angeles for tomorrow and forgot. That's the restaurant where Bella and Edward dine in the novel, remember? I flew down early to talk to the manager in person, to bribe him into giving us a table."

"Did it work?" Tanya asked.

"It sure did."

Tanya beamed at her. "Thank you, Ellen. That's so sweet—and an awful lot of trouble to go through. I'm so excited."

If Tanya only knew, Ellen thought.

"Didn't we say we wanted to order Bella's mushroom ravioli?" Ellen added.

"That's right," Sue confirmed. "So, tomorrow we start the *Twilight* tour in Forks and then drive to Port Angeles?"

"That's the plan," Ellen said.

Tanya clapped her hands. "I can't wait."

Ellen quickly looked up the restaurant on her phone hoping and praying that she could get a reservation for tomorrow. She asked Sue to pull into the next convenient store so she could use the restroom, and while she was inside, hiding from Tanya, she made the call. Ironically, her fictional account to Tanya came true when she had to beg the manager to squeeze them in at five, promising a bonus to the restaurant for accommodating her.

That evening, after dining on grilled king salmon at Lake Crescent Lodge, the three friends and Ellen's dog returned to the enchanted bungalow to watch the sunset on the porch overlooking the magnificent views.

"Isn't this the life?" Tanya said after a while. She'd been looking at the sea through binoculars.

"It certainly is," Ellen agreed as she pet Moseby, who was curled on her lap.

"Though it could be improved with our very own cabana boy," Sue pointed out. "Anyone up to making us a pitcher of margaritas?"

"I'll do it," Ellen offered. "After the sun sets."

"I'm scanning the horizon for whales," Tanya said, "But so far no luck."

"I hope you get to see one for your birthday," Sue said. "It would be a shame to come all this way and not."

"It would be a shame," Tanya agreed, "but even without the whales, this area is by far my favorite of all the places we've been together. I can't get over how beautiful it is here."

Ellen kicked off her rubber boots and pulled off her socks, to give her feet a chance to breathe. It was chilly out as the sun sank behind the horizon, and Ellen couldn't get enough of the cool weather. She sighed, wishing Brian were there with her to enjoy the views. Maybe the two of them would visit La Push another time.

"What on earth?" Sue cried, pulling Ellen from her reverie.

Ellen turned to Sue, who was staring down at Ellen's feet. "What's wrong?"

"Your toenails!" Sue said indignantly. "You should think about trimming those before your next pedicure. You're likely to draw blood!"

Curious, Tanya put down her binoculars to have a look. "I'm surprised you didn't put holes in the toes of your boots. Those look lethal—especially that snaggle-tooth one."

Tears filled Sue's eyes as she laughed so hard that she could barely breathe. "Oh, Ellen. I hope you weren't wearing sandals in Texas with those weapons exposed."

"Who cares about toenails?" Ellen asked defensively. "It's not like I took a dump in front of spectators." Ellen was referring to the time

Tanya went to the bathroom at the Pioneer Woman's studio behind a glass door, not realizing passersby could see her through the pane. "Or found a string of toilet paper leading from my butt to a bathroom down the hall in a bed and breakfast." That last comment referred to Sue.

"I don't know," Tanya said, also now with tears in her eyes. "Those look pretty bad. We may have made some embarrassing mistakes, but, Ellen, those toenails are on you."

Ellen didn't know what all the fuss was about. So what if she had long toenails?

"They're about to start curling on you," Sue spat, still unable to breathe.

"Come on, Moseby." Ellen ignored her friends. "Let's go make those margaritas. Maybe we'll put something special in them to shut these girls up."

"You aren't mad, are you?" Tanya asked.

Ellen shook her head. "I'm glad I was able to bring you so much joy on your birthday trip. Maybe I'll leave my toenails long since they provide you both with such high-level entertainment."

"No! Don't do that!" Sue squealed.

"They're just awful!" Tanya shrieked.

She listened to them laugh at her as she made her way to the kitchen with Mo. She could still hear their laughs over the sound of the blender.

When the silverware drawer opened on its own and a fork flipped out and onto the floor, Ellen said, "Don't you start with me, too. We have a deal, remember?"

The drawer closed. Moseby whined. Ellen bent over and tossed the fork in the sink, relieved to hear her oblivious friends still laughing but tempted, nevertheless, to throw the fork at them.

CHAPTER EIGHT

The Tour

After an uneventful night, Ellen woke early before the others, took Moseby for a short morning stroll around the bungalow, and then returned for a hot shower. The hot water felt good after the cold rain, but Ellen was too vexed over her promise to the ghost of Dan Pullen to relax completely. She still hadn't figured out how she was going to get out of this sticky situation. Truly, the only thing she could do was to dig up his body and salt and burn his bones—the sooner, the better.

But how would she manage that without alerting her friends? She'd have to come up with some excuse to get away. She needed to buy a shovel and gloves and gasoline. Oh, the thought of digging a grave all by herself in the dead of night filled her with dread, not only because of her fear of Dan Pullen's ghost (what if he were to find out?), but also because of the physical toll it would have on her body. Not in the best shape and approaching sixty, she wasn't all that confident that she could pull it off on her own. The last time she dug up her garden to plant a five-gallon transplant of confederate star jasmine, it nearly killed her. But should she risk hiring someone who might one day confess the crime to the authorities, no matter how much hush money she offered?

She considered confiding in Sue, but what good would that do? Sue was less capable with a shovel than Ellen. In fact, if anything, Sue would be a liability, unable to stand for long periods of time and certainly not able to dig more than two or three shovelfuls of earth without collapsing.

As if the ghost sensed Ellen's deliberations, the shower faucet turned off. Ellen watched in horror as the knob turned without her help. Feeling especially vulnerable without her clothes or a towel, Ellen jumped from the tub and wrapped herself in her terrycloth robe. Before leaving the bathroom, she had another shock. Written in the steam on the mirror over the sink were the words *You promised.*

Trembling, Ellen said, "It's only been two days!" Her voice came out more loudly than she'd intended. "We agreed on a week! Do you hear me? A week!"

A sudden knock at the door caused Ellen to jump.

"Ellen?" Sue called through the door. "Everything okay? Who are you talking to?"

Ellen cracked open the bathroom door to give Sue a reassuring smile. "I'm on the phone with a plumber. Don't mind me."

"A plumber?" Sue wrinkled her brow. "Is there something wrong with the pipes?"

"We have a leaky faucet at home," Ellen lied.

"Can't Brian handle it?"

Ellen looked into Sue's concerned eyes, wanting desperately to confide in her, just so she wouldn't feel so alone. While it was true that Sue couldn't manage a shovel, she was the best when it came to moral support.

And Sue could always be the lookout while Ellen did the digging.

"Ellen?" Sue studied Ellen's face.

Whispering, Ellen asked, "Where's Tanya?"

"She went for a walk."

Ellen glanced across the kitchen and living room and not seeing the birthday girl, grabbed Sue's hand and pulled her into the steaming bathroom before shutting and locking the door.

"What's going on?" Sue asked with a look of bewilderment. "Whatever you do, for God's sake, don't kiss me. I was kidding about wanting to be sister wives."

Ignoring the joke, Ellen pointed to the mirror.

"You promised," Sue read aloud. "Who promised what?"

Ellen suddenly realized that whatever she said to Sue would be overheard by the ghost.

"I promised someone I would do something," Ellen explained. "And you're going to help me."

Sue looked from Ellen to the mirror and back to Ellen again. "What are you talking about?"

"Don't say a word to Tanya. Let me get dressed, and I'll explain later. For now, just know that the ghost of Dan Pullen is still here with us."

"What?" Sue's brows disappeared beneath her bangs.

"You asked who I was talking to. Well, it wasn't a plumber, Sue. It was a ghost. Now, let me get dressed, and later I'll tell you all about what we're going to do to help him."

An hour later, they were on the road to Forks, an easy town to navigate since there was only one main road—Highway 101—running through it. Although the town was relatively flat and small, it was surrounded by gorgeous mountains. They drove from one end to the other as they headed to the Chamber of Commerce to pick up a *Twilight* map and to take photos with Bella's orange trucks.

As she drove, Sue said, "This is going to sound crazy, but do either of you sometimes forget that your mother is gone? I ask because I'm wondering if this only happens to me—something funny or interesting will happen, and my first instinct is to call my mom. Then I remember."

In the back seat beside Mo, Ellen frowned. "You were closer to your mom than I was to mine. I was always jealous of that."

"Me, too," Tanya piped in from the passenger's seat. "I used to be closer to my mother, before the Alzheimer's set in. For the last ten years of their lives, I was closer to my dad. Even now, I talk to him every day—Mom, too, sometimes, but mostly my dad. I sometimes forget that she's perfect now. I should talk to her more."

"I talk to my mom more now than I did when she was alive," Ellen remarked as a feeling of sadness swept over her.

"But neither of you think to call them?" Sue asked. "I guess it's just me."

"You used to call your mom every day," Ellen pointed out. "Old habits are hard to break. Plus, your mother's death is more recent than ours. It takes a long time to get used to. Oh, look. Bella's trucks!"

Sue pulled into the parking lot beside the orange pickup trucks and they snapped photos together before entering the Chamber of Commerce, where a young woman gave them maps and a brief description of their self-guided tour. Ellen and Tanya posed beside life-size cutouts of the *Twilight* cast while Sue took more photos.

Before they left the Chamber for their first stop, Tanya needed to use the restroom, and while Ellen and Sue waited for her in the car with Moseby, Sue prompted, "Okay, spill. What's going on?"

Ellen leaned forward so she could square herself to Sue. "It's been terrifying, Sue. Silverware flying at me and poor Moseby, doors swinging open and closed, and I think the ghost touched me on the back of my neck and maybe even laid in the bed with me!"

"What?" Sue's eyes widened.

"And you saw his threatening message in the steam on the bathroom mirror."

"You promised," Sue repeated. "What does that even mean?"

Ellen told her about the picture she had drawn while channeling Pullen's ghost.

"You promised to burn Oceanside Resort to the ground?" Sue asked in a voice at least an octave higher than usual.

"It was the only way I could get him to back off before you and Tanya got here."

Sue shook her head. "Why didn't you tell us not to come?"

"By the time I realized I couldn't banish him, you had already boarded the plane!"

"We can't burn down the resort, Ellen!"

"Well, of course not. But we can't let Pullen's ghost know that."

Tanya emerged from the Chamber and headed toward the Traverse.

"So, what's the plan?" Sue demanded.

"We'll have to dig up his body and salt and burn the bones."

Sue gasped and stared at Ellen with a look of incredulity. Before either of them could say anything more, Tanya entered the vehicle and they had to pretend as if nothing out of the ordinary were going on.

"So much for not having a bladder the size of a pea," Ellen said, thinking quickly. "Looks like you need more therapy."

"Try to get a man next time," Sue added before glaring at Ellen in the rearview mirror.

"Ha, ha, very funny," Tanya said. "Where to next?"

Ellen looked at the map. "The Swan House."

Although the white, two-story home didn't look exactly like the Swan house in the movies, Ellen thought it had a similar vibe and could see how it may have been the inspiration for the house in the book. Currently, it was being used as a bed and breakfast, so she and her friends weren't allowed to tour the inside, but cutouts of Edward and Jacob gazed down at them from the front upstairs windows, and a sign read that the place was being renovated by Esme and Alice.

They took a few photos and then continued to the community hospital, the high school, the police station, and the Cullen House—also a bed and breakfast closed for public touring. They posed by the mailbox, which read "The Cullen House," and then finished their tour at the Rainforest Arts Center, where they viewed props and costumes from the movie.

For lunch, they dined at BBG Blakeslee's Bar & Grill, which reminded them of the restaurant where Bella ate with her father. They each had a piece of mixed berry pie for dessert in Bella's honor.

Before leaving the restaurant, Ellen needed to use the restroom. With Mo in his cloth pooch carrier, she waded through the booths and tables to the back. Afterward, when she emerged from her stall, she was surprised to find Sue waiting for her in front of the sinks.

"Just how do you plan to dig up a body and salt and burn the bones without Tanya—or anyone else—knowing about it?"

When another toilet flushed, Ellen nearly had a heart attack. Their faces white, Ellen and Sue held their breath until a young girl, maybe twelve years of age, came out and ran from the bathroom without even washing her hands.

"Let's get out of here before she returns with her parents," Ellen urged.

As Ellen followed Sue from the restaurant, she noticed how quickly Sue could walk when properly motivated. When they reached the Traverse, where Tanya was already waiting in the passenger's seat, they put on their smiley faces.

"To Port Angeles?" Sue asked from behind the driver's wheel.

"Orcas, here we come!" Tanya sang.

Ellen was jealous of Tanya's ignorance and not too happy with Sue's scowl reflected in the rearview mirror.

They hadn't been driving for very long when Tanya looked up from her phone and said, "There was an orca sighting at Sekiu Point fifteen minutes ago! It's only a half hour out of our way. Do y'all mind if we go there now?"

"You're the birthday girl," Sue said. "I don't mind."

"Me either," Ellen added. "We still have plenty of time before we have to be there for our dinner reservation."

Sekiu Point was a small fishing village of colorful houses in blues, yellows, and reds set in the cliffside overlooking Clallam Bay and the

Salish Sea with the Canadian coast on the other side. Sue pulled into a parking lot near the harbor, where a few RVs were camped at the water's edge, and the three of them climbed out with Moseby to investigate the area.

Tanya used her binoculars to scan the sea while Ellen walked Moseby along the shoreline. Sue said she wanted to walk the few yards to the convenience store near the docks to grab a coke.

Ten minutes later, Sue ran outside waving for them to come over.

"I think that's the first time I've ever seen Sue run when she wasn't being chased," Tanya joled as she put her binoculars over her shoulder and began heading in Sue's direction.

"Me, too. Come on, Moseby-Mo, it must be important."

Ellen half-ran and half-walked behind Tanya, who cried, "What's wrong, Sue?"

"You have to see this!" Sue exclaimed. "Hurry!"

Once they caught up to her, Ellen and Tanya followed Sue around to the other side of the store where the ships were docked and to their great surprise, they saw three sea lions swimming in the harbor.

"The lady behind the counter said that they come every afternoon at high tide to eat the fish heads left by the fishermen," Sue explained. "Aren't they adorable? Look at those whiskers!"

Moseby barked excitedly, causing one of the sea lions to look their way.

"He's looking at us!" Tanya dug her phone from her pocket and held it up for a photo. "Got it! What a great picture!"

A fourth sea lion arrived and jumped onto the dock next to the store, only a few yards from where Ellen and her friends were standing. Mo had stopped barking and was watching the animals with fascination, his tail wagging.

"I'm taking a video," Sue said from behind her phone. "I want to send it to the kids."

"Oooh, good idea," Ellen agreed, fiddling for the phone in her purse.

"I'm so glad we drove by here," Tanya said. "I didn't get to see orcas, but these sea lions are so fascinating. Look at him eating! Isn't that cute?"

Ellen was glad to see Tanya enjoying herself on her birthday trip. It made all the hard work and ghostly drama worth it.

In Port Angeles, they parked near the visitor's center and walked across the long city pier toward an observation tower that was 150 feet high. While Sue opted to stay below on the pier, Tanya, Ellen, and Moseby climbed the steep stairs to the top to gaze out over the Salish Sea and the coast of Canada on the other side. Although they saw no orcas, they did see two otters playing along the shore of Port Angeles and eating from a kelp bed.

Once they were seated at their table at Bella Italia, Ellen and her friends ordered Bella's mushroom ravioli and glasses of red wine. Moseby hadn't been allowed to join them inside the restaurant, so he was in his plastic carrier in the back seat of the Traverse with a window cracked. The vehicle was parked on the curb in front of the restaurant, and Ellen could see it through the window from where she sat.

Suddenly, Tanya narrowed her eyes and glared across the table at Ellen. "Okay, girlfriend. Tell me what's really going on."

CHAPTER NINE

The Dead of Night

The return trip from Port Angeles was quiet. When they reached Forks, Tanya remained in the Traverse with Moseby while Ellen and Sue went into Forks Outfitters, to the hardware section, to look for two shovels, three pairs of gloves, three flashlights, batteries, and a can of gasoline.

"Just give her time," Sue reassured Ellen.

Ellen couldn't stop the flow of tears, even as the other shoppers glanced curiously at her.

"She's never going to forgive me," Ellen muttered through a tight throat as she dropped the work gloves into their shopping cart.

"Of course, she will," Sue said. "Once she gets past the deception, she'll realize what you've gone through to make her birthday special."

Ellen added the shovels to the cart. "You still agree that this is the right thing to do, don't you?"

"You and Tanya are right. If we leave when the week is up with your promise unfulfilled, we risk further endangerment to the tribe."

"It would be irresponsible of us. Plus, he could follow us home."

"Yes. I agree. Tanya does, too."

"We have no choice."

"So, let's get it over with."

Silence continued to dominate the vehicle as they drove to La Push. Tanya sat in the back seat with Moseby, her lips pressed into a thin line.

When they reached the bungalow, Ellen repeated, "You don't have to go with us."

Tanya heaved a sigh. "You can't do it without me."

Ellen knew Tanya was right. Of the three of them, she was the most fit, the most capable of digging the grave. But it was the last thing Ellen wanted her friend to do on her birthday trip.

Sue put the Traverse in park, and, without turning off the engine, said to Ellen, "I want to grab one of the chairs to take with us."

"I'll get it," Ellen volunteered.

Ellen ran inside and filled one of her totes with bottled water from the fridge before carrying one of the heavy chairs to the vehicle. Sue opened the back of the Traverse and helped Ellen to lift the chair inside. Then they climbed in and headed for the cemetery.

Before leaving Bella Italia, where they had enjoyed Bella's mushroom ravioli, Sue had Googled "Dan Pullen's grave Quillayute River" and had found the location on a site called *Find a Grave*. According to Google Maps, it was only sixteen minutes away from the bungalow at a place called Quillayute Prairie Cemetery, on the other side of the river, just as Mary the librarian had said. Google Maps hadn't revealed whether the cemetery was in an open place or a secluded one, and Ellen wasn't sure which she preferred. A secluded place was better for getting away with things; however, that was true for the ghost of Dan Pullen, too.

This wasn't the first time they'd been forced to dig up a body, but the last one had been the shallow grave of a child in the swampy ground of New Orleans. Ellen feared the limestone rock of the west coast would be nearly impossible to penetrate. She hoped the rain, which had begun to fall again, would make the ground soft and more penetrable. And more than that, she hoped that she and her friends could complete their mission without getting caught. Digging up a body on your birthday was bad enough; getting arrested and going to jail would be unforgiveable.

But worst of all, the fear of angering the ghost of Dan Pullen loomed. They must be on their guard and ready for a spiritual attack.

They took 110 back toward Forks but turned off on Mora Road, just past an RV park. Dusk gave way to night as they crossed the Quillayute River. The road soon narrowed and became lined with tall firs and cedars, obscuring views of anything but the dark road before them. Sue made one more turn onto Quillayute Road and, after passing a tiny air strip, emerged from the trees to an even tinier clearing that was the cemetery.

It was a square plot no bigger than 500 square yards and bordered on two sides by thick trees. Two roads converged to form the other half of the square, and a small black fence ran between them and the cemetery. On the opposite side of both roads were more thick trees.

So, secluded it was, Ellen thought.

Sue parked the Traverse beneath a cluster of trees on the side of the road. Ellen put Moseby on his leash and a pair of gloves on her hands and then, with her tote of water bottles on her shoulder, carried a flashlight and shovel in each hand while they searched the two dozen headstones for Dan Pullen. Although it was raining, it was just a sprinkle and not enough to diminish the visibility of the engravings on the tombstones.

Ellen made her way through the first row of graves, shining her flashlight on each headstone she passed. "We're fortunate it's a small place."

"I wouldn't call us fortunate," Tanya murmured as she put on the other pair of gloves.

Something about the resentment in Tanya's voice irked Ellen.

"Seriously?" Ellen snapped. "We found gold, struck oil, and saved countless souls, and you wouldn't call us fortunate?"

Tanya ignored Ellen and continued down the second row of headstones with her flashlight.

"To be fair, Ellen," Sue, struggling to keep up with them, began, "those things didn't just happen to us. We put our lives in danger and did our level best to solve mysteries that no one else had solved."

"We have millions between us," Ellen pointed out. "We are fortunate."

"I found it," Tanya said from where she stood beside an obelisk-shaped tombstone. "At least, I think this is it. It says D.W. Pullen."

"Don't say his name out loud!" Sue warned.

"Oops. Sorry." Tanya continued reading the headstone, "Born May 24, 1842. Died August 18, 1910."

Ellen carried her shovel toward Tanya. "That's it. I'll get started. Sue, can you hold onto Mo?"

Sue took the leash and shined her flashlight on the grave where Ellen began to dig.

"I'll go back and get the chair," Tanya offered. To Sue, she asked, "Is the vehicle locked?"

"No, just in case we need to make a quick getaway."

"Good thinking." Tanya turned to go.

After Tanya was out of earshot, Sue asked Ellen, "What is wrong with you, jumping down Tanya's throat?"

"How long is she going to punish me?" Ellen lifted a shovelful of dirt and tossed it behind her.

Sue shined her light where Ellen dug. "More than five minutes, I'd imagine."

Ellen stabbed the ground with her shovel again, thankful that the rain had made the soil soft. "Doesn't she get that I was thinking of her, trying to spare her feelings?"

"Is that really what you were doing?" Sue asked.

"What do you mean?"

"You could have been honest with her about forgetting our reservations. She would have been disappointed, but she would have forgiven you—eventually."

"You said she would kill us."

"In case you haven't noticed, I tend to exaggerate."

"So, you think I did all this—why? Because I didn't want to look bad to Tanya?" Ellen stabbed the ground angrily with her shovel.

"Or to yourself, maybe? You didn't want to feel like a bad friend."

"Am I a bad friend?" Ellen threw her shovelful of dirt with too much force.

"No, of course not, but sometimes you can get a little self-absorbed, especially when you're painting."

Tears sprang to Ellen's eyes. Tanya approached with Sue's chair and set it down for her. Sue took her seat and continued to shine the light for Ellen. Tanya took the other shovel and began to dig, too.

They were quiet for a while, except for the occasional grunt when one of them hit a rock with her shovel or struggled with dirt that didn't want to part with the ground.

But, after nearly an hour had passed, after they'd dug a hole about three feet deep and three feet wide, Tanya suddenly turned to Ellen and said, "Are we even friends?"

Ellen's mouth fell open as she used her foot to push her shovel into the earth. "Why would you even ask me that? Of course, we're friends."

"Friends trust one another, Ellen."

"Oh, gosh!" Ellen kept digging, worried someone would find them and report them to the authorities. "I promise to do everything I can to earn your trust again."

"I trust *you*. You don't trust *me*." Tanya threw a shovelful of dirt so hard that some of it hit Sue's chair.

"Careful there," Sue warned. "We're not here to bury *me*."

"I trust you," Ellen argued, unsure why her friend would believe otherwise. "I trust you with my life. Don't you know that?"

"Then why lie?" Tanya threw down her shovel.

"I wanted to spare you."

"You should have told me about the deal you'd made with Dan Pullen as soon as we arrived."

"Ssh. Don't say his name," Sue warned again.

Ellen kept digging. "I just wanted your birthday to be perfect"

Tanya glared at her. "If you wanted that, you wouldn't have forgotten to book our rooms."

"I'm sorry. I'm so sorry. I got distracted. I made a mistake."

"I forgive you, even if you don't trust me."

"But I do."

Moseby whined, and Sue cooed, "It's okay, Moseby."

"Then why lie to me?" Tanya demanded. "Maybe you don't think I can handle the truth? I'm a paranormal investigator, too, Ellen. I know my way around ghosts. I've been there right alongside you and Sue." Then she turned to Sue, who had picked up her shovel and was doing a sorry job of digging. "Oh, Sue. Give me that."

A set of headlights drew their attention from the ground.

"Flashlights off!" Ellen warned, grabbing her light from the ground and shutting it off.

Sue switched hers off while Tanya did the same.

Ellen held her breath as a car passed.

"We need to hurry and get the heck out of here," Sue said.

"I'm going as fast as I can," Ellen snapped again.

Once the car was out of sight, Sue flipped her flashlight on and held it for the diggers. "Let me know if you need a break. I can dig, too, you know."

Ellen sighed. Digging a grave the size of an adult was hard work, and it would be faster if Sue held the light and kept watch than if she tried to dig, too. They had marked off a rectangle for themselves but the deeper they went, the harder it was to keep the dirt they dug up from falling back into their hole. They found that they had to dig the grave in a wide circle to keep the sides of the hole from collapsing in on them. In the movies, the gravediggers always made perfect rectangles, but Ellen and Tanya were making a mess of it.

"If you could spread the dirt back, away from the hole, that would be helpful," Ellen said to Sue.

"I was hoping I wouldn't have to get my clothes dirty," Sue complained.

Ellen and Tanya, who were dirty from head to toe, looked at each other in disbelief.

"Kidding!" Sue sang.

They dug in silence for at least four more hours, only stopping briefly for water, before Tanya's shovel hit what sounded like the wood of a coffin. Ellen's back and shoulders were killing her. Their hole had become at least twelve feet in diameter at the top and eight feet in diameter at the bottom. It was warm down there, their heads below the level of the ground, beneath where Sue sat with Moseby shining her light.

"We're nearly there," Tanya told Sue. "God, I'm going to need a massage after this."

"I'll treat all three of us, if we make it out of this alive," Ellen promised.

"No need to be so dramatic," Sue remarked. "I think we'll make it out alive alright. But we might have to go to jail first."

"Don't jinx us," Tanya said to Sue.

"If I'm not at least ten pounds lighter after this," Ellen began, "then there's no hope for me."

"Shoot, I see another car," Sue said as she turned off the light.

Down in the hole, Ellen and Tanya were in near pitch darkness. Ellen got down on her knees and used her hands to scrape the last layer of dirt from the top of the coffin.

When Sue's flashlight turned back on, Ellen looked up.

"Everything alright up there?" Ellen asked.

"The car slowed down and freaked me out, but I don't think they saw us," Sue admitted. "How close are you?"

"Come on, Tanya," Ellen said, "Let's pry this sucker open."

They had to dig for another half hour to make enough room to stand beside the lid so the shovels would clear the sides of the hole.

"What's going on down there?" Sue demanded impatiently. "It's going to be morning before too long."

"This isn't as easy as it looks," Tanya said sarcastically.

Feeling delirious from sheer fatigue, Ellen laughed. "And we make it look so easy, don't we, Tanya?"

Tanya giggled. "I feel like I could collapse and die right here."

"Me, too. Just when I think we're almost done, we're not."

Ellen and Tanya wedged the tips of their shovels beneath the casket lid and used their full weight to pop it open. Ellen braced herself for a horrible stench and was pleasantly surprised when it didn't come. It must be the cold climate, she thought.

"Throw down the salt, Sue!" Ellen cried enthusiastically.

But when they pushed the lid all the way open, Ellen and Tanya gasped.

The coffin was empty.

CHAPTER TEN

Getaway

I can't believe it," Ellen groaned. "All that work for nothing. I'm so sorry, Tanya."

"You couldn't have known," Tanya reassured her.

Ellen was touched by Tanya's comforting tone. She'd expected her friend to be sore with her.

"What's going on?" Sue called from above.

"The body isn't here," Tanya explained. "It's just an empty casket."

"What do we do now?" Tears of frustration stung Ellen's eyes. Again, she said, "All that work for nothing! Where could he be?"

"Oh, my gawd!" Sue said. "Do you hear those sirens? What if they're coming for us?"

"Let's get out of here." Tanya quickly tossed her shovel to the ground overhead. "Take everything we brought back with us. We can't leave anything behind that will connect us to this crime."

Ellen clawed at the sides of the hole, but she couldn't pull herself up and out like Tanya had. The incline was too steep.

"Go on without me!" Ellen heard the sirens getting closer. "This is my fault anyway. Save yourselves!"

Moseby whined.

Tanya bent her knees overhead and held out her hand to Ellen. Sue was doing the same, but she was too short for Ellen to reach.

Ellen grabbed Tanya's outreached hand and quickly realized that the only thing it would accomplish would be getting Tanya back down into the hole. "You can't pull me up. I weigh twice as much as you."

Tanya jumped back into the hole beside Ellen and knelt on one knee and made a step out of the other. She slapped the top of her thigh and said, "Climb up."

"I'll hurt you."

"Dang it, Ellen. Trust me for once."

Ellen stepped onto Tanya's birdlike thigh and grabbed ahold of Sue's outreached hand before hoisting herself out of the hole with Tanya pushing her from behind.

Then Tanya climbed out and grabbed Sue's heavy chair and ran toward the Traverse, saying, "You guys get the shovels and flashlights. Hurry!"

As the sounds of sirens grew closer, Ellen and Sue huffed and puffed across the cemetery, each dragging a shovel. Moseby trotted alongside them, excited for what he probably thought was a fun game. It wasn't fun for Ellen, though. She prayed with all her might that she and her friends would make it out of the cemetery, into their rental, and out of the vicinity before the cops arrived. When they reached the vehicle, Tanya had already opened the back and had loaded the chair. She helped Ellen and Sue put the muddy shovels in, and then they scrambled inside.

With arms and legs covered in dirt, Ellen slid into the back seat of the Traverse with Mo. She had just closed the door behind her when the lights of sirens illuminated the road in front of her.

"Oh, my gawd! Our goose is cooked!" Sue cried as she started the engine. "Should I make a run for it?"

"No!" Tanya objected. "Running will only make it worse."

"She's right," Ellen agreed. "It's time to face the music. I'll tell them I forced you. I'll say I blackmailed you, threatened you."

As Ellen was trying to get her story straight, she watched in shock as a firetruck approached and flew past them and continued down the road. She and her friends gaped at one another. Then Sue started laughing and shrieking like a hyena—like a crazy, delirious hyena.

Tanya threw her head back and guffawed.

Ellen started crying and laughing at the same time. "What the heck just happened?"

"Thank you, God!" Sue shouted. "I promise to try harder to be good from now on. Thank you!"

"That won't last five minutes," Tanya teased, still laughing. "Now, come on. Let's get out of here."

"Should we close the casket and cover it up?" Ellen wondered.

"I don't have the strength for that," Tanya said. "Do you?"

Every bone in Ellen's body ached. "No. Let's go."

Sue turned the car around and headed back toward La Push. Ellen passed out water bottles, which were surprisingly cold and tasted delicious. After she had consumed an entire bottle of water, she poured some in her hand for Mo. Although her body was covered in dirt, the gloves had kept her hands relatively clean. Moseby was thirsty, too, and lapped up the water eagerly.

As they neared 110 on Mora Road, they saw the lights of the firetruck ahead. Ellen stared at the smoke billowing up past the canopy of fir and cedar trees lining the road, shuddering at the memory of the sketch she'd drawn while channeling the ghost of Dan Pullen.

"An RV is on fire," Tanya spotted from the passenger's seat when they neared the scene.

"Oh, no." Ellen leaned forward. "I hope no one was killed."

Sue slowed down as they passed. Campers, young and old, stood wrapped in blankets watching as firefighters worked to put the fire out and stop it from spreading to other RVs and surrounding forest.

"Should we stop and help?" Tanya wondered.

Sue laughed. "Looking the way we do, covered in dirt?"

"Yeah, I guess not," Tanya said. "I just hope everyone's okay."

"It looks like they have a lot of help," Ellen pointed out. "And every inch of my body hurts."

"Mine, too," Tanya admitted. "I don't know what I was thinking."

Sue smiled at Tanya. "It's your instinct to help others in need."

"We need to figure out what to do next," Ellen mentioned once the fire was behind them. "Where could he be? Why wasn't he where he was supposed to be?"

Sue turned onto La Push Road. "Do you think that librarian might know?"

"I don't think so. She's the one who told me he was buried there."

"Someone has to know something," Tanya mused. "He's bound to have descendants who know."

Sue shook her head. "It might look suspicious if we call them up and say, hey, we dug up your ancestor's grave and found it empty. Can you tell us where he is?"

Ellen giggled. "Yeah. That wouldn't reflect well on us."

"*We* dug up your ancestor's grave?" Tanya repeated while smiling at Sue.

"Hey! I moved the dirt, held the light, and kept watch," Sue reminded her. "And I'm just as dirty as you are—well, maybe not quite. You've got it in your hair, and you smell worse than I do."

"Thanks," Tanya said dryly as she shook her head and chuckled.

"You're welcome," Sue teased. "Always glad to help, however I can."

Ellen chuckled, too, then she quickly added, "Don't forget that we can't talk about this at the house or anywhere on the grounds, okay? If the ghost discovers what we did—what we tried to do—well, let's just say he won't be very happy with me."

"What if he knows?" Tanya asked in a worried tone. "What if he already knows?"

Ellen had been wondering the same thing.

"I guess we're about to find out," Sue said as she turned up the hill toward the enchanted bungalow. "Be on your guard, ladies."

Moseby looked at Ellen, as if he understood the gravity of the situation as well as anyone.

Sue put the vehicle in park, and everyone climbed out. The bungalow appeared to Ellen as it had that first night—barely visible except for the dim circle of the porch light. Hadn't they left on any lights?

Before walking through the front door, Ellen turned on her flashlight. "We come in peace."

"Let's leave our muddy boots on the porch," Sue suggested. "In fact, you two might want to strip before going inside."

Tanya kicked off her boots. "I can't wait for a hot shower."

Ellen tugged at one of hers. "You go first, since you're the birthday girl."

"No, that's okay. You go and test the waters, so to speak. I'll sit out here and wait my turn."

"What makes you think it's any safer out here?" Sue asked Tanya.

"I have an idea!" Ellen said suddenly. She returned to the vehicle, her legs beginning to cramp on her. "Let's let him know what we tried to do tonight."

Sue and Tanya exchanged looks of confusion as Ellen returned with the can of gasoline.

"We went to burn down Oceanside Resort," Ellen announced into the house from the porch. "We took a can of gasoline. See? But someone almost caught us. We fell in the mud as we got away. We'll try again later. Just leave us in peace for now, okay?"

Sue and Tanya took Moseby to the back porch to wait while Ellen stripped outside and then walked in her stockinged feet to the bathroom to shower. As good as the hot water felt moving down her sore body— which she knew would be even sorer tomorrow—she couldn't relax knowing that the ghost of Dan Pullen was probably watching her. She quickly got out and dried off, put on her robe, and hurried out through the kitchen door, her back already stiff and one of her hips cramping up.

"Who's next?" she questioned her friends.

"Go ahead," Sue said to Tanya.

"Thanks." Tanya stripped out of her dirty clothes, leaving them in a pile on the porch, and then in nothing but her bra and panties, made her way to the bathroom for her turn in the shower.

"I'll get dressed and come back out here to sit with you and Mo," Ellen said to Sue.

"We'll be right here," Sue said. "But don't leave us alone for too long."

"I'll be right back. Promise."

Ellen made her way to the stairs, her back seizing every now and then, but she stopped short when she heard Tanya scream.

"Tanya?" Ellen rushed to the bathroom and pulled open the door.

Tanya stood in her underwear pointing with a shaky hand at the mirror.

Ellen followed Tanya's finger and gasped. Words written in the steam read, "I know what you did."

Ellen covered her mouth. There was no way around it. She had betrayed the ghost and he knew it.

"What do we do now, Ellen?"

"You didn't write those words, did you, Tanya?"

Tanya narrowed her eyes at her. "Of course, not."

"I wouldn't blame you, after all I've put you through."

"Ellen, I didn't write those words."

Ellen had hoped she'd been the butt of a mean joke. A girl could hope, couldn't she?

"I believe you," Ellen finally said. "I'll stand guard while you shower off. I promise not to leave you alone."

Tanya climbed into the tub and pulled the curtain closed. Ellen remained vigilant while she silently prayed to God for protection, clinging to the *gris gris* she wore around her neck.

Tanya asked from behind the shower curtain, "Are you still there, Ellen?"

"I'm still here."

"I'm nearly done."

Once she was finished and was in her robe, Tanya warned Sue about the message in the mirror. Then she and Ellen stood guard while Sue showered. Moseby joined them.

Afterward, the ladies quickly parted ways to get dressed. Then, they met in the living room to come up with a plan.

"We'll take turns keeping watch," Sue decided. "Since you two are exhausted from digging, I'll take the first shift."

"The sun's coming up," Tanya pointed out. "Maybe he won't be as active during the day."

"Let's hope that's the case." Ellen doubted Pullen's spirit needed the energy from the moon and stars to launch his attacks. He'd already demonstrated amazing power with the silverware.

"Let's make a circle of protection around Tanya's bed," Sue said. "I'll bring in one of the chairs from the porch."

"How long can you stay awake?" Tanya asked as she followed Sue into her room.

"Two hours, I think. Is that good?"

"You're just going to sit there for two hours without falling asleep?" Tanya asked. "That's hard to believe."

"There's no way I'm falling asleep in that chair. As comfortable as it is, it's not *that* comfortable. Plus, I have a book in my room—a good mystery I've been reading."

"I'll take the second watch," Ellen offered while Sue went to get her book.

Ellen poured the salt while Tanya dragged in a chair. Then, Ellen sprayed more holy water throughout the room. Sue returned with her book and a blanket from her bed and made herself comfortable in the heavy chair. Then they said the words together to close the circle, which encompassed most of Tanya's room.

Guardians of the North, South, East, and West,

Elements of Earth, Air, Fire, and Water,
Bless this circle and protect those within,
Whether father, mother, son, or daughter.
No unwanted entities shall enter,
And safety shall prevail in the center.
This circle is cast.
Grant it shall last.

Before letting Mo on the bed, Ellen wiped him down with her wet towel. Then she and Tanya climbed on the bed with him between them.

By now, Ellen's entire body felt like one big cramp, and she wished she'd taken some ibuprofen before attempting sleep. But now that she was already laying down, she didn't have it in her to open the circle of protection, find the bottle of pills, take them, close the circle, and climb back into bed. Just thinking about it made her want to cry again.

Instead, she curled her arm around Moseby, taking comfort in the warmth of his little body and in the softness of his fur, and prayed to God to protect them as they tried to get some sleep.

Ellen felt rested when kisses from Mo awakened her. Bright sunshine filled the room, and the cries of seagulls could be heard just outside the French doors. Ellen blinked and attempted to stretch, but her muscles cramped, and a painful charley horse overtook her right thigh. She took a deep breath and tried to relax, tried to calm herself. After a minute, the cramp loosened. She was surprised her fit hadn't awakened Tanya.

She looked over at Sue's chair and found it empty, the circle of salt on the floor unbroken. Sue must have opened and closed the circle behind her. Ellen climbed out of bed with Moseby in her arms and did the same. Then she put Mo down on the outside of the circle, and he followed her as she went from room to room, gently calling for Sue.

When Ellen found no sign of her friend, she opened the front door to find the Traverse gone. Sue had left them alone with the evil ghost?

What had she been thinking? If Sue left because she had a hankering for doughnuts, Ellen would kill her.

Ellen quickly went back to Tanya's room, found her phone charging on the nightstand, and called Sue.

She heard Sue's phone ringing from across the house. Ellen followed the sound to the bathroom, where Sue's phone was sitting on the back of the commode.

Tanya appeared in the bathroom doorway. "What's going on?"

"Sue's gone, and she left her phone behind."

"She never leaves her phone behind. It's practically attached to her hand."

"Exactly. So, where is she?"

CHAPTER ELEVEN

Too Close for Comfort

Hoping that Sue had made a doughnut run and would return at any moment, Ellen said to Tanya, "Want to join Mo and me for a morning walk? I don't want to leave you here alone with you-know-who."

"Aren't you sore? I can barely move." Tanya emptied the coffee pot into the sink and washed it out.

"Oh, I'm sore alright. But Mo has needs."

"I have needs, too, and right now I need coffee, so you go on, assuming you won't be gone long."

"No. And we'll be right outside. But I thought hot tea was your choice of beverage."

"Not when I'm *this* tired."

Every muscle in Ellen's body protested as she followed Mo through the kitchen door, across the back porch, and to the grassy hill. She wondered where the nearest spa was and how soon she could book three full-body massages. She also wondered how much ibuprofen a person could take without poisoning herself.

The breeze felt good against her cheeks and the sky was unusually sunny today as she and Mo made their way along the side of the hill. The ocean sparkled in the sunshine as the waves washed toward the sandy shore below. Mo tugged, wanting to go down to the beach, but there was no way Ellen could handle the climb today.

"Sorry, Moseby," she said. "We're not going far."

The sun was at high noon. Had she and Tanya really slept for six hours? Why hadn't Sue woken Ellen after two hours, as planned?

Ellen continued to enjoy the views of the ocean, the elephantine rocks, the petrified logs, and the tree-fringed islands. The condos of Oceanside Resort, which were fully booked but always appeared quiet and vacant, had a parking lot full of cars this afternoon. There was a family getting out of one of them. The adorable, little girls in pigtails made Ellen miss her own grandkids.

Suddenly, Ellen squinted as her heart raced in her chest. Parked next to the family in the parking lot was a black Traverse. It looked exactly like *their* Traverse. It was even muddy on the back, like theirs had been the previous night.

Ellen led Mo to the porch, where she found Tanya's binoculars to have a closer look at the car.

"What the heck?" Ellen whispered as she zoomed in on the vehicle. "It *is* ours!"

Ellen knew it was *their* Traverse because of the unmistakable, muddy chair leaning against the back windshield.

Why was their Traverse parked down there? What was Sue up to?

"Tanya! Come quick!"

Tanya emerged through the back door. "What's wrong?"

Ellen handed over the binoculars. "Is that our Traverse parked in front of the condos down there?"

"Why would our car be down there?" Tanya took the binoculars and put them to her face.

"It's it, isn't it?"

"Oh gosh, it is! But why? Wait, is that Sue in the driver's seat? Oh, my gosh, Ellen, she's slumped over the steering wheel!"

"No, it can't be." Ellen grabbed the binoculars with shaky hands and zoomed in on the driver's side window. Sue's profile, like the muddy chair, was unmistakable.

"Oh, no." Worry coursed through Ellen's veins. Sue looked as still as a corpse.

"What if she's hurt?" Tanya worried. "We better get down there right away."

A pit formed in Ellen's stomach as she imagined the possibility of Sue dead. She refused to think about it as they quickly dressed and put on clean shoes before rushing down the steps to the beach with Mo on his leash. Ellen groaned with every step down the steep hill, as her hips and legs cramped and her back seized.

"Oh, God, please let Sue be okay," she prayed aloud as she followed Tanya, who was surprisingly quick given how sore she was.

Moseby was the only one in a good mood as they rushed past the graveyard of dinosaur bones, toward the condos, and to the parking lot behind them.

Tanya tried to open the driver's door but found it locked. Pounding on the driver's window, she said, "Sue? Sue? Are you okay?"

Relief swept through Ellen when Sue lifted her head and gazed at them with a blank look on her face. Her forehead was swollen like a goose egg and had blue and green streaks bruising through it.

"Open the door!" Tanya insisted.

Sue opened the door and blinked. "What's happening?"

"You tell us," Ellen said, trying to keep Moseby from investigating the parking lot. "What are you doing down here?"

Sue glanced around and then winced with pain. "Ow, my neck."

"Your head doesn't look good either," Tanya observed. "Climb out, and let Ellen drive us back to the house, where you can tell us what happened."

Ellen and Tanya helped Sue from the driver's side to the back seat. Then Ellen put Mo in the back with Sue and climbed behind the wheel. She was about to push the ignition button when she stopped to adjust the rearview mirror.

"Do I smell gasoline?" Tanya asked as she climbed onto the passenger's seat.

"I smell it, too," Ellen said.

"Oh, my gawd!" Sue cried out. "Don't start the car! Everybody out. Out of the car!"

Ellen and Tanya exchanged looks of confusion.

"Sue, what the heck is going on?" Ellen demanded, not budging from her seat.

"I remember what happened." Sue struggled from the back seat and helped Moseby out, too. Then she backed several feet away from the vehicle with Mo in her arms. "I thought it was a dream. Look, there's the can of gasoline on the pavement. I'm sure it's empty."

Ellen and Tanya jumped from the vehicle. Ellen's back seized, and she groaned with the pain.

"I dreamt that I was you-know-who," Sue recalled. "I got the gasoline can from the porch and drove it down here. I poured it all over the vehicle and made a line of it to the condos, to the bottom of those stairs. Then I got into the car, where I planned to start the engine and blow myself up and the car with me."

Sue started crying as Ellen and Tanya tried to process what she had revealed.

"I can't believe I nearly killed myself." Sue trembled. "I need to sit down."

"I came this close to starting the ignition just now," Ellen murmured. "Sue, are you sure?"

"That was my dream. How else can you explain why I'm here?"

"Did he possess you?" Tanya asked with wide eyes. "Are you possessed?"

"I don't know." Sue rubbed the back of her neck. "I'm not sure what happened."

"You must have hit your head on the steering wheel and passed out," Ellen speculated. "Maybe that's why the ghost couldn't control you after that."

"What do we do now?" Tanya wondered. "Should I call 9-1-1?"

"We should call the Quileute police," Ellen said. "There's a totem over there, across the parking lot, in front of the resort office. They'll know what to do. We can tell them the truth. They know about you-know-who."

"I'll go," Tanya offered. "What's the number?"

"It's there on the totem by the phone. You'll see it," Ellen assured her.

As Tanya left, a couple emerged from their upstairs room and made their way down the steps toward the parking lot. Ellen's mouth fell open when the man pulled out a cigarette and lit it.

"Wait!" Sue cried. "Don't light that!"

It was too late. The man took a drag and smiled down at them. "It's a free country."

"You don't understand," Ellen pleaded. "It's not safe."

The man arched a brow and took another drag before blowing the smoke toward the two friends.

"Please, listen to us," Sue shrieked, backing further away from the vehicle with Moseby.

As Ellen tried to explain the situation, the young man ignored her. He took another drag from his cigarette and smiled again at Ellen as he reached the foot of the stairs between the condos and the Traverse.

"I'm not trying to be rude," Ellen explained. "It's dangerous. There's gasoline . . ."

The man smiled once more before dropping the butt on the sidewalk in front of her.

Flames immediately engulfed him and, a split second later, the Traverse. Ellen jumped away from the flames and landed on the sidewalk on her hip.

Two hours later, Ellen sat with Tanya on stiff chairs near the foot of Sue's bed in a private room at Forks Community Hospital. Two young officers, one Quileute and the other Forks, were interrogating them about what had happened. Sue had been admitted because of a concussion. The doctor wanted to keep her overnight for observation. While the hair on Ellen's arms had been singed and her hip was badly bruised from her fall, the muscle cramps from a night of gravedigging had injured her far more than the fire. Moseby, who'd been with Sue at a safe distance away from the explosion, sat on Ellen's lap in his cloth pooch carrier. The young man with the cigarette was down the hall in the Intensive Care Unit. Ellen was anxious to hear the most recent update on his condition.

"And you admit to dowsing the SUV with gasoline?" the Forks officer was asking Sue.

"Like I told Officer Pullen during the drive over," Sue began, "I vaguely recall doing it. I was sleep-walking. I would never have done such a thing otherwise. It was all a dream to me."

"A nightmare," Ellen corrected.

"And you hadn't been drinking or taking any drugs?" The Forks officer asked.

"No, sir," Sue replied.

"They tried to warn the smoker," Tanya pointed out. "Don't forget that part."

"True." Ellen nodded. "I was frantic, but he wouldn't listen to me."

"He thought we were judging him," Sue said. "He sure showed us."

"Sue," Ellen chastised. "He's fighting for his life down the hall."

"I'm just saying . . ."

"I've got what I need," the Forks officer verified. "I'll be in touch."

Officer Pullen, who had already explained that he was not a descendant of the white settler by the same name, remained behind. Younger than the Quileute police officer named Hobucket who'd given Ellen a key to the bungalow twice, Officer Pullen appeared to be in his late twenties or early thirties. He had driven the friends from the resort to the bungalow so Sue could get a change of clothes and so all three could retrieve their purses before heading to the hospital. During the drive over, he had listened to them talk about the flying silverware that had attacked them as they'd run in and out of the bungalow, and he'd asked them not to mention it to the Forks officer.

"I've just got one more question," Officer Pullen said.

Ellen lifted her brows. "Yes, Officer?"

"The can of gasoline. Why did you have it in the first place? Were you worried about running out?"

"Um." Ellen exchanged looks with her friends. "Well, you see."

"You aren't very good at this, Ellen," Sue said. "Just tell him the truth. He's Quileute. He'll understand."

Ellen glanced at Tanya, who nodded.

Then Ellen swallowed hard before saying, "We were planning on salting and burning you-know-who, er, Dan Pullen's remains. That's why we had the gasoline."

The officer's mouth hung open, and he gazed at each of them with a look of incredulity on his face. After the shock wore off, he asked, "Did you?"

"We tried," Tanya admitted. "But the casket was empty."

"You hired someone to dig up the grave?"

"We did it ourselves," Ellen said. "At Quillayute Prairie Cemetery. We went there last night with every intention of banishing his ghost. But it was all for nothing."

"That must have taken you quite some time."

"All night," Tanya said.

The officer shook his head and sort of whistled.

"There was no body?" he asked.

"There was no body," Ellen confirmed. "You wouldn't happen to know why?"

The officer whistled again and shook his head.

Ellen lifted her finger. "Do you, by chance, know how we can reach Mary the librarian? Maybe you know the number to the library?"

"Mary Pullen?" he asked.

"Is she related to you?" Sue wondered.

"She's my grandmother."

Ellen supposed she shouldn't be surprised. It wasn't like the tribe was very large in numbers. "Oh. Well, you see, I was hoping to ask her advice about what's been happening at the bungalow. We could use her help."

The officer scratched his chin. "I have a feeling the entire tribal council is going to want to talk to you about this."

A nurse poked her head inside the door. "You still doing okay, Miss Sue?"

"My head and neck hurt. Can I have morphine?"

The nurse laughed. "I highly doubt it, but I'll ask your doctor." Then she noticed Moseby. "I'm sorry, but pets aren't allowed inside the room, unless they're a patient's service animal."

"He *is* Sue's service animal," Ellen blurted out without thinking.

"Oh?" the nurse arched a brow with a suspicious gleam in her eyes. "Really? Where are his credentials?"

"Um, they were in the rental car before it went up in flames," Ellen said as blood rushed to her face. Why was she telling such boldface lies? She supposed she was afraid to leave Sue's side with the possibility that Dan Pullen might be possessing her, but she couldn't bear to be parted from Mo, either.

"And what's the nature of his service to Miss Sue?" the nurse inquired.

"Diabetes," Ellen bluffed. "He can sense when her sugar level is too low."

The nurse went to the foot of Sue's bed and had a look at her chart. "I don't have diabetes listed in your medical history."

"It's controlled by medication," Sue lied with a worried glance at Ellen.

"I'll make a note," the nurse said. "I'll need the name of that medication, along with the dosage and frequency."

Sue put a hand to her head. "I'm having trouble remembering that at the moment."

"No worries. I'll get your medical history from your regular doctor soon. The fax should be coming in at any minute now. Meanwhile, I'll let the kitchen staff know to send up only diabetic meals while you're here."

"Awesome." Sue glowered at Ellen. "I'm looking forward to that."

Once the nurse had left the room, Officer Pullen said, "Okay, ladies, you've answered my questions for now. I have your contact information if I think of anything else. And I'll let you know when a meeting with the council has been arranged. We have our drum circle tonight. I'll update the tribe and get back with you. Here's my card if you think of anything else."

"Thank you, Officer," Tanya replied, taking the card.

Alone in the room with her friends, Sue groaned, "Diabetic meals only?"

Ellen sighed. "I'll buy you Ding Dongs from the vending machine down the hall."

"Promise?" Sue asked.

"Promise," Ellen repeated. "But first, we need to call Father Yamamoto from Santa Fe. I'm afraid you may need to be exorcised, my friend."

CHAPTER TWELVE

A Makeshift Exorcism

W hile I live and breathe!" Father Yamamoto said to Ellen over the phone. "Hey, you heard about our sleep-walking nun, didn't you?"

"What? No, Father. That's not why I'm calling," Ellen explained.

"Yeah, we call her a roamin' Catholic, ha-ha!"

Ellen grinned and rolled her eyes. "You sound well, Father Yamamoto. And just so you know, you're on speaker."

"It's good to hear your voice. How are Sue and Tanya?"

"Hi, Father," Tanya greeted. "I'm fine."

"I've been better, Father," Sue announced from across the room.

Ellen glanced at Sue in her hospital bed. "That's why I'm calling. How soon can you come to Forks, Washington to perform an exorcism on Sue? Can you fly out today?"

"An exorcism? Oh, dear. What makes you think she's possessed?"

Ellen told the priest about their near-death experience.

"How frightening," the priest exclaimed. "If only I could help you. I have two funerals and a wedding this week. Isn't there a local priest who can assist you?"

Ellen glanced at Tanya. "Possibly. We'll ask around."

"If not, you can perform the exorcism, Ellen. I wouldn't recommend this to just anyone. You, however, I've seen in action. You have the gift."

Ellen lifted her brows. "Me? I don't think so. I don't know how."

"Sure, you do. You were there. You did as much as I to help Ruth. Your friends, too."

"Thank you for that last part, Father," Sue said. "I was beginning to worry that you'd forgotten the part that Tanya and I played."

"Never! You ladies were fantastic!"

"I recall we used incense to purify the room and to protect us from possession," Ellen said, "but we're in a hospital, and I don't think I can burn anything in here without setting off the fire alarm."

Tanya shook her head. "There's no way."

"You can use sound to cleanse the room," the priest said. "You can use it to cleanse Sue, as well."

"Sound?" Ellen glanced at Tanya, who shrugged.

"You've seen the mass, haven't you? You've seen the altar boys ring the bell during the consecration of the host?"

Ellen bit on her lower lip. "Um, I suppose so."

"Bells, cymbals, rattles, drums—all have been used to clear negative energy and to purify spaces and people. Use prayer and intentions in combination with sound, Ellen. Do you have a bell? If you don't, they are usually carried in hospital gift shops for this very purpose."

"Really? I've never heard of that."

Tanya shrugged again.

"Remember to tether her to the bed," Father Yamamoto continued. "Her strength will surprise you, if she is, indeed, possessed."

Ellen glanced around the room for something to use to bind Sue to the hospital bed. "My dog's leash could work."

"Sounds kinky," Sue said with a laugh.

"The leash would work perfectly," the priest said. Whether he hadn't heard Sue's comment or was just ignoring it, Ellen wasn't sure. "You have a dog?"

"His name is Moseby. He's a rescue my husband found."

"What a blessing. And do you still have some of the holy water I gave you?"

"Yes."

"If Sue is possessed, it will likely cause a rash, possibly boils, so use sparingly."

Ellen shuddered and glanced again at Sue. "Will do."

"Then pray. That's really the meat of any exorcism, Ellen."

"I don't know the words, Father."

"Speak from the heart. Ask God to remove the ghost from Sue's body. Pray for the soul of the ghost, that it repents and reconciles with its maker. Pray for Sue's purification. You can do this, Ellen. I'll be praying for you."

"What if it doesn't work? Or what if things go wrong, like that time that woman died on you?"

"You're in a hospital. If she struggles to breathe, call for the doctor, okay?"

"Oh, my gawd," Sue moaned nervously.

"Okay, Father Yamamoto. Thank you for your help."

"Call me and let me know how it went. I'll be praying for you."

"Thank you."

"By, Father," Tanya said.

Ellen ended the call and glanced nervously at her friends. "Let's do this, ladies."

"You don't think we should find a local priest?" Tanya asked.

Ellen shrugged. "Go for it, Tanya."

"Guys, I'm not possessed," Sue insisted.

Ellen stood up from her chair and gave Sue a stern look. "That's the same thing Ruth Okada said."

While Tanya searched on her phone for a priest, Ellen and Mo went to the gift shop in search of a bell. Ellen had never heard of sound used as a purification tool, but she hadn't heard of most of the things she'd learned in recent years, since becoming a paranormal investigator.

She was surprised to find that Father Yamamoto had been right about the bells in the gift shop. A row of tiny, white, ceramic bells with

Forks Community Hospital printed on them were in a prominent place near the cash register. Ellen picked one up, gave it a little ring, and, satisfied, put it on the counter to purchase.

"Anything else?" the young woman behind the counter asked.

"Do you have any Ding Dongs and maybe a cherry coke?"

When she returned to Sue's side, Ellen thought she'd been mistaken for an angel of God. The way Sue looked at Ellen with gleaming eyes and joyful smile caused Ellen to turn and look behind her, to make sure Jesus himself wasn't standing behind her. She quickly learned it was the Ding Dongs and coke that had Sue's eyes gleaming.

"Thank you," Sue said as she opened the package and stuffed one of the Ding Dongs into her mouth. "Mmm. I needed this."

"We better get a move on," Tanya noted. "Visiting hours are almost over."

"I was hoping to stay the night," Ellen said. "Where else would we go? All the motels are booked, remember? Unless you want to risk sleeping in the bungalow tonight."

Tanya frowned. "Not after what happened to Sue."

"One of you can sleep on the couch," Sue said. "I suppose we can ask for a cot, too."

"Or we can sleep in shifts," Ellen proposed. Then she asked Tanya, "Did you find a priest?"

"No. I guess it's up to us."

Ellen unhooked Mo's leash, which she had curled beside him in his cloth pooch carrier, and tied one end to Sue's headboard. "Put your arms over your head."

"Can't I finish this cherry coke first?"

Ellen sighed. "Take another sip and finish it after. Then you won't have to share it with you-know-who."

"Ha, ha, very funny," Sue said dryly before taking another sip from the cold aluminum can.

Ellen put the can on the bedside table and then tied Sue's wrists together with Moseby's leash.

"This isn't very comfortable, Ellen. Are you sure this is necessary? My neck and head are killing me."

Ignoring Sue, Ellen said, "Tanya, you do the holy water while I ring the bell, okay?"

"I don't know about this." Tanya hesitated as she took her bottle of holy water from her purse. "But okay."

Ellen rang the little ceramic bell. "I cleanse this room and its people." She glanced down at Moseby hanging across her body in his cloth pooch carrier. "I mean its, er, inhabitants, of all negative energy. Evil spirits, fly away, never to return."

"Don't get it in my eyes," Sue said to Tanya, who leaned over her face dribbling water from the bottle. "That's cold. Do you have to use so much?"

"Watch for a rash," Ellen instructed.

"Sue, were these pimples here already?" Tanya pointed to bumps along Sue's hairline. "Or did this holy water cause that?"

"They were there already. Come on, girls, this is ridiculous. I'm not possessed!"

Ellen shook her head. "Oh, no. Her personality is already changing, just like Ruth Okada's." Then in a louder voice, Ellen said, "I beg our almighty God to take the soul of Dan Pullen from the body of Sue Graham. Help the evil ghost to reconcile with his maker."

"This is insane!" Sue shouted. "Tanya, you're getting it in my nose!"

"Leave her body, Dan Pullen!" Tanya belted out. "Leave our friend Sue Graham alone!"

The heads of all three friends turned when the door to the hospital room opened and Sue's nurse, wearing a look of horror and consternation, said, "Excuse me! What on earth are you doing to my patient?"

"We're exorcising her," Ellen explained. "We think she's possessed."

"Ladies, I need you to step away, or I'm going to have to call security."

Tanya and Ellen stepped back while the nurse unfastened the dog leash from Sue's wrists and headboard before handing it over to Ellen. "By the way, Miss Sue's paperwork came through, and, as I suspected, she has no history of diabetes. I need you to remove the dog from the premises."

Just then, Officer Pullen and his librarian grandmother, Mary, entered the room.

"Everything okay in here?" the officer asked.

"We were trying to exorcise Dan Pullen from our friend," Ellen said to the Officer. "Mary! So good to see you! Can you help us?"

As the librarian moved closer to the bed, the nurse said, "And I was just asking these ladies to remove their dog. They lied about him being Miss Sue's service animal. She doesn't even have diabetes."

"Is that true?" the officer asked Ellen.

"I don't have anywhere to take him," Ellen explained. "I didn't mean to cause trouble."

"This woman is not possessed," Mary said of Sue.

Tanya and Ellen exchanged looks of skepticism.

"How do you know?" Tanya asked.

"From experience. I can see with my mind's eye. Can't you?"

Ellen still didn't have faith in her ability to see with her mind's eye. It was all so new to her.

"I told you," Sue declared. "Gawd, what you two put me through. I nearly choked to death on holy water."

"I guess that wasn't a personality change after all," Ellen murmured to Tanya. "It was just plain ol' Sue getting mad at us."

"I nearly choked to death!" Sue said again.

"Ma'am, I need you to remove the dog," the nurse insisted.

"Hello, Moseby." Mary pet Mo where he was curled in his cloth pooch carrier. "I suppose I could keep him for you."

Ellen curled her arms protectively around her dog. "Thank you, but I can't be parted from him. It might trigger his PTSD."

"Then what are you going to do?" Tanya asked. "You can't stay here if you keep Moseby."

"You're welcome to spend the night in the jail," Officer Pullen offered. "You and the dog can both stay. You'd have a cell to yourselves."

"What about the other prisoners?" Sue wondered.

"There's only one—our village drunk, old man Walker. And he's harmless. He sings. He's pretty good, too."

Ellen frowned. "I don't know. A jail cell?"

Her back still hurt from the night of gravedigging, and the thought of a cot was not too appealing.

"She and the dog can sleep in the back room of the library," Mary offered. "There's a couch. It'll be comfortable enough for one night."

Ellen lifted her brows. "Really? Oh, thank you so much."

During the drive from the hospital to the library, Ellen rode in a pickup in the middle of the bench between Officer Pullen and his grandmother librarian. Ellen held Mo in his cloth pooch carrier in her lap.

"Was there a reason you came to see us at the hospital?" Ellen asked Mary. "It wasn't to offer me and my dog a place to stay."

"I told her about the grave," Officer Pullen answered. "About there being no body."

"Do you have any idea where he might be buried?" Ellen asked Mary.

"No. I came to warn you," Mary said.

"Warn me?"

"Jackson is going to notify the press about the grave being vandalized," Mary revealed.

"Jackson?"

"That's me," the officer added. "And don't worry. I won't name any names."

"But why?" Ellen furrowed her brows. "I don't understand why you'd want to involve the press."

"Maybe they can find out the truth from Dan's descendants," Mary explained. "We need to know where his remains are resting. He isn't where he's supposed to be, and that could be the reason he's stuck on that hill."

"I see." Ellen felt as if all that digging, and all her sore muscles, hadn't been for nothing after all. If the reporters could pressure Dan's descendants into revealing where he was buried, maybe the tribe could finally get some peace.

"Do you need anything from the bungalow?" Officer Pullen asked as he neared La Push.

As much as she wanted to pick up her toothbrush and a change of clothes, she was too afraid of what might be waiting there for her. She and her friends had barely dodged the flying silverware earlier. She asked if they would stop by the general store instead, so she could buy a few things, including dog food.

On the short ride from the store to the library, Ellen asked, "If Pullen isn't your ancestor, how is it you came to have the same surname?"

"It was easier for the Indian agents and the schoolteachers to assign our ancestors names they could pronounce," Mary explained. "I guess the names stuck."

"Does it bother either of you?" Ellen began, "having the same last name as the man who posed the greatest threat to your tribe's survival?"

"It bothers me," the police officer maintained. "But it's been in my family for decades. It would dishonor my family not to keep it."

Mary shook her head. "Names aren't good or evil, people are. And people rarely think of themselves as evil. Hitler was the hero in his own story. Dan Pullen felt the same."

"How could he?" Ellen said. "How could he possibly justify his actions?"

"You should read his journals," she suggested.

"You have them?"

"At the library. Would you like to read them?"

Ellen's eyes widened with surprise. Would she like to read them? "Absolutely!"

CHAPTER THIRTEEN

Dan Pullen

After feeding, watering, and walking her sweet Moseby-Mo, Ellen made herself comfortable in the back room of the musty library on a sofa beneath a beautiful, handmade blanket. Stacked on a coffee table nearby were four leather-bound journals with the handwritten account of Dan Pullen's life. Mary had left Ellen with a warm cup of tea and a bright reading lamp before returning home for the night. Ellen sat with Moseby curled beside her and cracked open the first journal.

***

I received this beautiful book of pages, handsomely bound in quality leather, from a new friend by the name of A.J. Smith, whose family, emigrants from the east like me, I helped during an unfortunate time. I had taken my schooner to Cape Flattery to trade furs and had stopped in at Neah Bay, where the new Indian agent, a standoffish man younger than me by the name of Willoughby, had just replaced old Huntington, and he told me the sad news of a family of his acquaintance. The father, my new friend A.J. Smith, had just been relieved of his services at the agency due to the change in administration, but before he had been able to find new employment, he and his wife and seven of their eight children came down with typhoid fever. They lost a young daughter on Christmas night, and the mother's life was still in jeopardy when I arrived in early February of 1878.

I remained with them for four days, staying up with the sick most in need of my services, and gave them cans of fruit, beef broth, and mutton, since they had exhausted their pantry. It did not take long for me to learn of their dire circumstances. Having just moved from the Dakotas to teach at the Makah school in the employment of the Indian Agency, A.J. was now without income, without land, and without a plan, as he and his family were still recovering from the loss of a beloved child.

I convinced him and his wife, Mary Jane, a stout woman with a kind face, to bring their family south with me to Quillayute, where there was plenty of land for homesteading. Having arrived there ten years prior with my brother Mart, and being the first white men in the vicinity, we found the native people, who are called Quileute—though they call themselves Kwo'liyot'—to be cooperative and eager to trade. Nomadic and reliant more on seal, salmon, and whale hunting than on agricultural pursuits, they haven't settled the land. They prefer their arduous adventures on the water to the domestic lives of white men, leaving the bulk of the area ripe for settlers to make a good home for themselves and their families.

Before continuing with my tale of how I came to know the fine and honorable A.J. Smith, a man who, like me, lives a temperate life without the need for alcohol or tobacco, believes in women's suffrage and the abolition of slavery, along with hard work and self-determination, I should offer a brief account of the events in my life preceding this fortuitous friendship, to make my record complete.

I was born in Maine, North America, in 1842, to a millwright, Daniel Pullen, for whom I was named, and his wife, my mother, Mary Ann Dudley. When I was but seven years of age, scarlet fever ravaged my family, taking my father and my older sister, and leaving two of my siblings completely deaf and me partially so. My unfortunate mother was widowed with eight surviving children under the age of thirteen, but she managed to keep us fed and sheltered and in school, though I also worked as often as I could. The oldest son, I grew up helping at the sawmills and would have been content to remain with my family if my mother, upon my eighteenth year, had not prevailed upon me to take to sea to avoid being conscripted into service for the Union Army.

This is something I have kept secret, for I am painfully ashamed. My mother depended on my income to feed my siblings, and still depends upon it, for I send her money every month. My death would have meant more than her heartbreak. It would have jeopardized the livelihood of our family.

Even so, I carry the shame with me like a deadly illness I wish to keep secret from the rest of mankind, and it is particularly painful when I meet an honorable man, like my new friend A.J. Smith, who served the Union Army bravely. I doubt I shall ever confess this shameful truth to him.

In the summer of 1860, I landed in Seattle and worked as a bull puncher at a Port Gamble logging camp. I was joined three years later by my younger brother Mart. We pooled our savings to purchase a pilot schooner in 1865, when we relocated to Neah Bay and operated a business ferrying captains to and from their ships. Not long after, I began trading for elk horn, sealskins, and the skins of mink, martin, muskrat, cougar, deer, and bear with the natives. The schooner enabled my brother and I to get top dollar for our goods along the Strait of Juan de Fuca and Puget Sound. The natives traded for sugar, tobacco, matches, fabric, and other manufactured goods. Mart and I settled on a fern prairie by 1868, where we built a house and a barn and began raising sheep. A few years later, we had enough money to send for the rest of our family, but only our brother Ephraim and sister Abbie—both of whom were married with young children—came. Mart and I helped them to clear land just up the river from us, build homes, and settle in.

In April of 1878, A.J. accepted my invitation to join me on the Quillayute prairie after putting his family on a steamer for Olympia, where the children could attend school. He lived with my brother and me for six months while we helped him prepare land for homesteading. The dense carpet of fern that clothed the prairie grew as high as ten feet, and the only way to combat it was by burning it. However, the land was flat, the soil fine, and the prairie without many trees, making it easier to cultivate for planting. In less than a week, we had planted 450 apple trees, 300 plum sprouts, and fifteen cherry sprouts, along with a wheat and kitchen garden. By August, Ephraim joined Mart and A.J. and me in building a log house for A.J. measuring eighteen feet by twenty-four feet and eleven logs high.

In early September, A.J.'s family returned from Olympia to Neah Bay, and I took the schooner to meet them and to bring them to their new home. I had trading in Port Townsend, where we were laid up by a storm, and six weeks later, I delivered the family safely to their new house, where A.J. was eagerly waiting with presents for all, including me. He gave me this very book.

As I expected, my new friend has proved to be a great addition to our settlement, for he immediately helped to establish a local paper, organized a Sunday School rotation at his home and the homes of two other families, and solicited the government to approve a postal route from Clallam Bay to Quillayute. Just recently (March of 1880), he was commissioned as postmaster, duties he took on in addition to teaching at the Makah school, writing articles, farming land, and raising cattle.

In December of 1879, A.J.'s daughter Hattie, who had been working as a cook at the Neah Bay Agency, left her job and was caught in a storm on her way home. For six days, her whereabouts were unknown, until her brother Wesley, a teacher at Neah Bay, learned that her boat had waited out the storm in the lee of Tatoosh Island near the tip of Cape Flattery. She eventually made it back to Neah Bay, where she remained with her brother Wesley, until her brothers Olly and David could fetch her on horseback. The group didn't arrive home until the middle of January, but Hattie insisted on having a Christmas tree party and inviting the neighbors, including my brother Mart and me.

I had first encountered Hattie's strong will when she was sick with typhoid and all her hair had fallen out, and she had refused to stay in bed. Her determination to celebrate Christmas with her family—even in January—further imprinted her in my mind as a person who, like me, meant to control her fate by sheer will. And unlike those fitful nights when she was bald and wracked with fever, the healthy, young woman, pink from days of horseback riding in the sun, had fiery red hair that fell to her shoulders and a fiery temperament to match. I daresay, I was struck dumb in her presence.

In February, I helped to build a second floor to the Smith house so Hattie could have a room of her own. It wasn't unusual for me to help. A.J. and I traded favors often. I plowed for him. He delivered my wool to the river landing for me. I helped with the mail sack, and A.J. used my sled to mow and haul his hay. He milked my cows when my brother and I were away, and I attended his Sunday school classes. Hattie might have suspected that my eagerness to build her room was motivated by more than friends swapping favors. If she did, she hid her suspicions well. When the room was finished, I helped her move her things up into it. She had two paintings on canvas of the local landscape, and I recognized James Island and Little James in one of them. When I asked her who did them, she smiled widely and said she had and offered me whichever I liked best. I could tell she preferred the one with the islands, so I chose the other—the coastline along Neah Bay.

By March, Hattie had proved herself a capable horsewoman. She drove cattle and herded sheep as well as anyone. By that time, I was installed at the new trading post, built by Baxter Fur Company, who had hired me as manager. I delighted in seeing Hattie come and go on her favorite gelding, Babe, riding side-saddle, the long strands of her fiery red hair pulling loose from their braids as if they wished to be as wild and free as she.

One afternoon, she stopped into the store after riding back from Neah Bay, her blue-gray eyes troubled as she combed the shelves, looking for something. There was a quality inexpressibly delightful in her determined expression. I felt I could have stood there watching her all day, but alas, I asked if I could help her find anything, after which she proceeded to burst into tears. She'd found an abandoned bear cub half-starved in the woods on the outskirts of Quillayute, and she was hoping I had one of the new bottle feeders. She had tried to bring the cub back with her, but it had been just big enough and fast enough to escape her efforts. It was her plan to take cow's milk to lure the cub into her arms and to calm its cries.

I never wished for something I didn't have as I did in that moment, for I hated to see that beautiful, hopeful, determined face altered by bad news. I told her to show me where she had last seen the cub and I would bring it back for her and give it milk from my own dairy cow. The joy that came over her features made my skin sweat and my heart pound like a native drum against my ribs. I mounted my horse and followed her to the woods, but the cub was nowhere to be found. We searched the whole afternoon until dusk had long settled and cold night blanketed the earth, and I had come to fear that it had been eaten by wolves. I accompanied Hattie home, our spirits dashed. After I left her, I resolved to find the cub if it were still alive. With lantern in hand, I mounted my horse and returned to the woods, and just as dawn broke over the horizon, I heard the cries of the cub.

Holding the cub in the crook of my arm as it clawed and kicked about, I pulled the cow's teat and directed her milk into the bear's mouth. The clawing and kicking ceased, the suckling began, and the bear was happy with me from that moment on, even if my poor dairy cow was not.

When I delivered the cub to Hattie later that morning, carrying it in my arms like a newborn babe, she expressed her pleasure and gratitude to me with a kiss on my cheek. Never have I felt happier than I did in that moment. I resolved to devote myself to undertaking every means possible to give Hattie Smith whatever her heart desired.

Hattie continued to care for the cub throughout the spring and summer, and it followed her around like a dog. Just today (September 20, 1880), I saw him climbing the trees on the edge of the prairie while she dug up potatoes. She playfully refers to him as our baby, a phrase that makes my heart pitter-patter with joy, because she wouldn't say such things if she didn't mean to lead me on. This evening, as I helped her carry her baskets of potatoes to the house, she told me my blue eyes were deeper than the sea, and without thinking twice, because I had already been thinking about it for months, I asked her to marry me. She dropped her baskets and threw her arms around my neck and made me the happiest man in the world.

A.J. and I just returned from Seattle (February 26, 1881), where we each spent two months' worth of earnings on wedding gifts for Hattie. He bought a gilt locket pocket Bible with a clasp, six place settings of silverware (the fanciest I have ever seen), along with two napkin rings monogrammed HSP. I bought bedroom furniture, a rocking chair, dishes, and glassware.

When I asked A.J. why he had chosen such expensive silverware, he said that a man's success can be gleaned by the daintiness of his spoon. Consequently, I bought more silverware.

   ***

Ellen looked up from the page and shuddered. Even after death, Dan Pullen had a thing for silverware. She wondered if the set in the bungalow was the same one that he and Hattie's father had purchased in Seattle so many years ago.

She turned the page and found she had reached the end of the first journal. Unlike modern diaries, the paper was thick, and because it was also small—measuring about eight inches long and six inches wide—it didn't take much to fill it up. Dan's large, looping handwriting, though easy to read, could fill up a single page with one long sentence.

But so far, his verbose and overly complicated sentences were the only flaws Ellen saw in Dan Pullen. How had a man kind enough to care for a family he'd never met while they suffered from typhoid fever become the evil villain who had burned the Quileute village to the ground? How had such a man nearly killed Ellen and her friends?

Ellen returned a missed call from Brian before texting Sue and Tanya to let them know she was settled. Then she sent a text to each of her children, saying she loved and missed them. By the time she had finished, it was ten o'clock. Since she wasn't sleepy, having slept until noon, Ellen picked up the second journal and opened it.

***

It is a perplexing yet joyful wonder to me that life has flown by faster in the past two years than in all my other years combined. Hattie and I were married on February 28, 1881, and a year later, our most precious Mildred, whom we call Dolly because she looks like a baby doll, entered the world. For the first two years, our sweet family lived in a wing of the store, where I continued to manage the trading post for Baxter Fur Company.

But a month ago, in March (1883), we moved into the house we built on our homestead on 160 acres of Quillayute Prairie, just up the river from A.J.'s property, and have begun cultivating the land for planting. We shall live here for the required two years to legitimize our claim but have already found the journey back and forth across the river to the store and home to be taxing, especially with a little one in tow, so yesterday I made a Preemption claim of 153 acres of oceanfront land at La Push near the store. Sitting over forty feet above sea level on a hill that juts into the ocean, it has breathtaking views of the water and James and Little James Islands.

In February, my brothers and I drove the cattle to slaughter, and today, I just returned from an unplanned trip to Seattle, where I had no choice but to give up our bear, Baby, to the zoo. He had gotten too big for us, and now that Dolly has begun to walk on her own and cries to go outside, we couldn't risk having the two in the same yard. We were afraid that Dolly would provoke him.

Hattie and I are both sad to see him go. I've promised her that we will visit him often at the zoo. We have put Hattie's painting of him on the wall by the kitchen. Even now, as I write these words, I am overtaken by emotion. He was our first baby, will always be our first baby, and the one that brought us together.

An unfortunate sequence of events has unfolded on our otherwise idyllic prairie. The wolf population has grown severely beyond its food supply. There is no more slinking into the fields at night to pick off a sheep or steer like thieves in the dark in a pack of two or three. These animals, some of them as large as a Newfoundland dog, have of late numbered in the dozens and as many to fifty in a pack. In the light of day, they come brazenly into the fields where the cattle are grazing, and they circle the one, usually an old and weak bull, who has wandered away from the herd. More than once of late, I have ridden upon such a spectacle to find the eyes of the poor bull eaten from their sockets, his tongue bitten off, the gristle of his nose completely gone, his ears but fur matted with blood, and the skin of his forelegs dangling like the strings of a faltering kite as his devourers encircle him.

To chase off the wolves to free their victim has meant their almost immediate return and the inevitable death of their prey. Shooting one or two of these wolves does not deter the rest of the pack from returning within hours for their singular objective. Yesterday (October 9,1883) at dusk, I did something I could not have imagined as a young boy my older self conceiving. I slaughtered a pig, salted its carcass with strychnine, and dragged it out to a field we aren't using for grazing. This morning the bones of the pig were surrounded by three dozen dead wolves. It was a sorry sight, an image that will be forever emblazoned on my eyes, and such a waste of life.

My beautiful Hattie is many things: she's a diligent mother, a dutiful homemaker and wife, a skilled horsewoman, a capable farmer, a determined hunter and angler, a talented artist, and a gifted cook and baker, making the most delicious pies I've ever eaten. She often helps at the store and with her father's mail sack. But I have told her that she cannot go on like this, working so laboriously from morning until night—and frequently through the night with our Dolly— especially now that she is pregnant again, and so we will hire servants from among the Quileute— perhaps a maid and a cook.

I love this time of year. Spring has arrived, and with it, new life. Hattie and I made a trip to Neah Bay today (March 20, 1884), where we visited with her brother Wesley, bought clothing and shoes for our family, and delivered mail for A.J.

Hattie looks fine in her new hat.

We have been haying for the past three weeks and now have such an abundance of potatoes this year (September 1884), and as Hattie is too pregnant to bend over, I've hired a crew of natives to help me, promising them half of what they harvest. Dolly and two little Quileute girls follow me around, helping to dig up the crop—a family affair indeed. We will keep some of what we harvest for ourselves, but after the Indians get their cut, the rest will be hauled out for trade. However, hauling the baskets along the trail to the river exhausts even the strongest of workers, so we cleared the land wide enough for a wagon. Within one week, at least a dozen others have utilized the path for the same purpose, and it has now become a veritable road.

Dolly loves chasing and being chased by the Quileute children in the fields and sitting on the ground with them making dirt pies. Hattie and I have observed that Dolly knows more of their words than ours.

Never have I felt more helpless than in the last ten hours. We are now in the fourth hour of the new year (1885), and I am gutted and joyful and wretched and humbled and many other emotions besides.

Hattie went into labor in the late morning on the eve of the new year while returning with Sam, our Quileute cook, and Sam's young son, Jonnie, from the store for provisions for what was to be a party to ring in the new year. Sam's wife, Rachel, who cleans for us, remained behind with Dolly. When Hattie arrived at the store, I scolded her for making the journey in her condition when I could have easily brought the goods home, but she insisted that she and Sam needed more time to prepare for the festivities. Although irked with me and my objections, she was otherwise well, and I knew nothing of what had transpired on their journey home until I arrived home myself just before dusk, around half-past six.

I learned that Hattie had gone into the pains of labor during the canoe ride across the river. Her screams had alerted many of the Quileute people, some of whom hopped into their canoes and followed Sam to the shore closest to our house on the prairie. Among those who followed were Sam's parents—Howeattle, the tribal chief, and Mama, a shaman and midwife eager to help Hattie during her delivery. But Mama soon discovered, once Hattie had been carried into the house and onto her bed, that the baby was breech and in need of turning. The process of turning a breech baby is dangerous in and of itself; however, even I know that only one in three women delivering a breech baby ever survives. By the time I arrived home to the sounds of my wife's exhausted wails and groans, Mama and Rachel had been trying to turn the baby for six hours.

Hattie lay on our bed writhing and wailing, her skin pale and clammy, her red curls wet and clinging to her face, and her eyes wild with fear. I took her hand and asked Mama if there was medicine that might help the pain, but Mama shook her head as she and Rachel continued to kneed Hattie's hard round belly as if they were trying to pound stone into dough.

Sam and his father, Howeattle, and the other men that had helped to carry Hattie inside were out near the barn smoking and watching Dolly and Jonnie running together in the yard.

"Don't push," Mama said to Hattie.

"I have to," Hattie sobbed. "It's killing me."

I took Hattie's hand and stared in horror as she bore down with all her might. The frightened glances between the Quileute women made my stomach lurch.

"Will everything be alright?" I asked them.

They ignored me.

A few moments later, Hattie bore down again, this time screaming the most blood-curdling scream I've ever heard, and that's saying something. I've heard all manner of wildlife scream with the agony of pain in death. I've heard men scream, too, after being shot or dragged or killed with an arrow or injured when their boat smashed into the rocks.

Mama reached down in between Hattie's legs and pulled like she was dragging an enormous salmon from the river. Hattie screamed as her flesh ripped and blood dripped onto the towels between her and the bed.

The women spoke anxiously in their native tongue.

"What are you saying?" I pleaded with them.

Hattie closed her eyes, became whiter than a sheet, and fainted.

"Hattie? Hattie, please don't leave me, my love!"

Then Mama pulled again, and this time she held my son in her arms. Unlike the cries of his mother, his cries brought tears of joy.

"He's good," Mama said. "Healthy boy."

"What about Hattie?" I asked.

Rachel held a bottle of something near Hattie's face and fanned the pungent odor into Hattie's nose and mouth. Hattie coughed and opened her eyes and looked at me in a way she had never looked at me before. Even when she was a bald kid suffering from typhoid fever, she'd looked more alive.

"Don't leave me, Hattie," I begged again. "We have a beautiful bouncing boy."

Hattie screamed again as the women pushed on her.

"What are you doing?" I shouted. "Leave her alone!"

"The afterbirth," Rachel explained. "It must come out."

Hattie fainted again, and I nearly did, too, but later, after Mama had applied an ointment on Hattie to soothe her torn flesh, we woke Hattie up and gave the baby to her to nurse.

"Let's call him Daniel," I suggested. "Is that alright with you, Hattie?"

She nodded. "Dee for short. Dolly and Dee. Where's my Dolly?"

"She's playing with Jonnie outside," Rachel said. "Sam is with them. Don't worry."

"You did good," Mama told her. "You strong woman."

"Thank you," Hattie said. "I couldn't have done it without you."

CHAPTER FOURTEEN

The Pullen Castle

Wednesday morning, Ellen awoke to the sounds of doors opening and closing and of other movements nearby and was momentarily confused as she glanced around the room, at the couch, and at Moseby curled in the crook of her legs. Then she remembered the library, La Push, the ghost of Dan Pullen, and the journals.

She had begun to suspect that there had been two Dan Pullen's: one who had written the journals and another who had burned down the Quileute village.

The door to the back room opened, and Mary poked her head inside. "Good morning."

"Good morning." Ellen sat up and combed her fingers through her short, dark-blonde hair. Her back was still very sore and stiff. She tried to stretch her arms, but even that hurt. "Thanks again for letting me stay here."

"Did you sleep well?" Mary entered the room.

"I did. Thank you."

"Jackson will be here in a minute to give you a ride to the hospital. Would you like some tea?"

"Jackson doesn't have to do that," Ellen said. "I can get an Uber. But tea sounds lovely."

Mary busied herself at the kitchenette across the room. She used a microwave to heat the water because there wasn't a stove.

"How far did you get in the journals?" Mary asked.

"Hattie has just given birth to their second child."

"Oh, so not very far."

"I thought I'd made good progress. I'm nearly halfway through them, I think." Ellen moved Moseby from the blanket and then folded the blanket and put it aside on another chair.

"Do you plan to finish?" Mary asked as she stood by the microwave waiting for the water.

"I'd like to. How did they come into the possession of your people, by the way?"

"They were donated to us many years ago by a great granddaughter of Pullen's who was wracked with white guilt."

Ellen's cheeks turned pink. "White guilt?"

"That's what she said when she gave them to me nearly fifty years ago."

Ellen wasn't sure what to say to that. "I need to check on my friends, to see when the doctor plans to release Sue. What time is it? I should give them a call."

Ellen looked at her phone and disconnected it from the new charger she'd bought the previous day at the store in La Push. It was already eight o'clock. She had a text from Sue saying to text or call her because Tanya's phone was dead.

Mary added tea bags to her tea pot and allowed them to steep while she rinsed the teacups that had been stacked in a drain board beside the sink.

"I'll be just a minute," Ellen said to Mary as she phoned Sue.

"She's alive," Sue said by way of greeting. "I wondered if we'd ever hear from you again."

"It's only eight o'clock."

"Ten o'clock our time. I've been lying here for hours. They're discharging me as we speak. Do we have a plan?"

"How's Tanya?"

"She's okay now that she's had some caffeine. I don't think she slept well last night. Our nurse came in every two minutes, it seemed."

"You won't believe what I've been up to," Ellen said.

"Don't tell me. You had a sordid affair with a handsome Native American."

"Sue!" Ellen glanced up at Mary just as Mary handed her a cup of hot tea. She hoped the librarian-shaman hadn't overheard Sue's comment. "No. I've been reading the journals of Dan Pullen."

"*Our* Dan Pullen? The evil ghost who tried to kill us?"

"It's hard to believe, but yes. So far, he seems like a stand-up guy. Something must have happened to him. He didn't start out evil."

Ellen glanced up at Mary who was taking a sip of the hot tea.

"That *is* hard to believe," Sue agreed. "I'd love to take a look at them."

"Why don't you and Tanya take an Uber over here, and we'll read them together?"

Ellen glanced up at Mary again, who nodded. It was a library, after all. Ellen supposed it was okay to hang out there and read.

"Tanya says she's starving, and my diabetic breakfast wasn't even good enough for Moseby."

"They gave you diabetic meals even after we came clean?"

"I guess they wanted to punish me."

"Then Uber to the River's Edge Restaurant, and I'll meet you there," Ellen decided. "We can return to the library after breakfast."

Over plates of waffles and French toast—the most non-diabetic meals one could order—Ellen told her friends what she had read so far in the journals of Dan Pullen. All three of them looked a bit rough around the edges, especially Sue, whose goose egg had flattened but had left behind a black and blue ring in the center of her forehead, resembling a third eye.

After breakfast, they took Moseby for a walk in the cool smattering of rain, before heading to the library, where they sat at the conference table, each with a hot cup of tea supplied by the hospitable Mary.

Since there were no other patrons visiting the building, Ellen read aloud from where she had last left off, after the birth of the Pullen's second child in January of 1885.

"'The plans for our future house arrived by mail today (April 1885). While honeymooning four years ago at Port Townsend, Hattie fell in love with the ornate Victorian homes that dotted the landscape. I vowed to her then that I would build a home even more spectacular than they. The floorplan boasts a parlor, dining room, kitchen, pantry, office, and lavatory on the first floor and three bedrooms on the second. Our room will be directly over the parlor, capturing the best view of the sea, observed through a luxurious bay window. In addition to the floorplan, the packet includes elevations, building instructions, and millwork cross section patterns.'"

Sue sighed. "Is the whole book as boring as this? Please tell me there are juicy parts."

"He tends to be a bit dry and verbose," Ellen admitted. "But the transition from good to evil is bound to have juicy parts."

"Good point," Sue admitted. "Keep going."

"Maybe I'll skip over some of these details about their spring planting, summer shopping, and fall harvest," Ellen said, as she scanned through Dan's lengthy sentences. "Okay, here we go: 'My brothers and I began construction on Hattie's dream house today (September 29, 1886), made easy with wood that had been precut and framed in Seattle. The cruciform structure took little time to lay out. The framing is nearly complete.'"

"Still boring," Tanya complained.

Ellen skimmed through the pages, looking for something relevant.

"This is interesting. He writes, 'I pay twenty-five cents a day to members of the tribe to carry water from the Dickey River to keep my tank full.'"

"It's really not," Sue said. "Get to the part where he goes postal."

"Okay, let's see." Ellen skimmed. "They had a second son named Royal in 1887. They began taking boarders for extra income but mainly because Hattie loved to entertain and show off the house. Hmm. This is interesting: they opened a room in their house to educate the children of settlers, because they weren't allowed to attend the Indian school. They added another wing to the house to serve as an official post office, and Hattie became commissioned as postmaster. That's cool, right?"

Tanya shrugged. "Yeah, I suppose."

Sue sighed. "Give me that. Apparently, you don't know what we mean by juicy parts."

Sue took the journal and skimmed the pages herself. She frowned.

"What?" Ellen asked.

"This is just sad," Sue began. "He's describing the wreck of a ship on the rocks in front of his house and how bodies keep washing up day after day. He writes how he and his wife and brothers cleaned the bodies and buried them in his field and notified the papers."

"Does that sound like an evil man?" Ellen challenged.

"He tried to kill us," Sue pointed out. "Just give me a minute, and I'll find where he changes."

Ellen took a sip of her hot tea and waited, but it wasn't long before Sue said, "This isn't juicy, but it's interesting, because I didn't know this. Dan is complaining about the tribe disputing his fence, arguing that the U.S. agreed to pay twenty-five thousand dollars over twenty years to the tribe for the land while the tribe retained hunting and fishing rights on unclaimed territory. He says the government also provided a school, a blacksmith, a carpenter, and a physician to aid native peoples. He writes, 'I have followed the letter of the law in claiming my homesteads, and yet Doctor Obi, a powerful shaman feared by many in this area, beat the hell out of me when I asked him to move off my land to the beach, where the other Quileute live.'"

"That is interesting," Tanya said.

Ellen glanced across the room at Mary, where she sat behind the wide desk apparently reading.

Sue continued, "Oh, then here, he writes, 'When I asked Sam why Obi thought he could get away with attacking me, Sam said that the chiefs had been misled in the 1856 treaty. He said they never intended to sell the land, only to allow settlers to share it with them. He said they never would have given up the prairie, because they depend on the cam-as that grew there and the deer and elk and other animals that graze there. The prairies, he said, belonged to everyone, and my fence en-closed the best parts. I told Sam that it wasn't my fault that the chiefs misunderstood the terms. I had obeyed the law. I told him to tell his friends that if anyone else attacks me, they'll have hell to pay.'"

"Maybe this is the beginning of the change," Tanya speculated.

"That's the end of the second journal," Sue said as she reached for the third. "Hopefully, we'll find our answers soon. We still haven't fig-ured out where we're sleeping tonight."

"Maybe we should rent a car and go to Seattle," Tanya suggested.

"We'll go back for our things, won't we?" Sue asked. "Good clothes are hard for me to find in my size, and most of mine are in the bunga-low."

"I left my good makeup there, too," Tanya said. "I'd hate to have to replace it."

"Ellen's expensive equipment, too," Sue added. "We don't want to leave that behind."

"Does this mean we're giving up?" Ellen straightened her back. "I thought we were going to stay and investigate."

"I assumed we'd let the tribe work it out," Sue said. "Didn't you say they're looking for Dan's remains? That may take a while."

Ellen bit her lip and tried to hide her disappointment.

Sue opened the journal and glanced over the first page. "This one begins with another row with the Indians. Dan writes, 'I came home today to find my wife holding a rifle on the trading post balcony. It was pointed at a band of Quileute, to whom she was shouting in their language. I picked up on some of it but got the full report after the band had dispersed. Hattie's brother Wesley, the teacher at the new Indian school here in Quileute, which operates out of a building I claimed and now receive rent on from the Indian Agency, had whipped a boy for misbehaving. The Quileute went to the school and surrounded Wesley and his assistant, Miss Bridget, and they might have been killed then and there if Wesley hadn't persuaded the mob to allow him to take his assistant home first. He promised to talk to them at his place, which is the room where Hattie and I once lived over the trading post. He went in and returned with his pistol and was able to hold the angry natives off for a spell. But then one of them grabbed the gun from him and was about to strike Wesley with the end of it when Hattie came out on the balcony and railed at them with her rifle.'"

"Good for her," Tanya said, before remembering that Mary was listening. "I just mean she sounds like a strong woman, defending her brother like that."

"While it's true that we don't know what Wesley did to the boy," Sue began, "I doubt he deserved to be killed over it."

The three friends stole surreptitious glances at Mary, whose poker face gave nothing away as she continued to read.

Sue scanned the next few pages. "Here Dan writes about farming and picnicking at James Island."

Ellen cocked her head to the side. "Tanya, didn't you say that's where the Quileute used to lay their chiefs to rest in canoes up in the trees, that it was sacred to them?"

"Yes," Tanya said.

"I doubt that went over well with the Indians," Sue whispered.

"I wouldn't think so," Ellen murmured with another glance at Mary.

"Okay," Sue said, sitting up in her chair. "Here we go. Dan writes, 'The Quileute have complained about me to the new Indian Agent, Oliver Wood, for demanding that they either pay rent or tear down the houses built on my land. Wood wrote to me stating that the Department of the Interior had issued an order in the spring of 1884 prohibiting settlers from filing claims on land occupied by natives. I wrote back explaining that I filed my Preemption claim in July of 1882, having already settled in the area in 1880, and submitted my Final Proof and payment in July of 1883, all before the new order. I explained that I put a great deal of money into building an extensive house for my family and have dwelled in it for over a year. Wood wrote back saying that because my patent has not yet come through, my claim to the land is unclear. I was so angry that I could have killed someone.'"

Ellen and her friends exchanged glances.

"That sounds more like the Dan Pullen we know so well," Ellen said.

Sue lifted a finger in the air. "Listen to this. Dan writes, 'I have gone to extensive and excruciating lengths to build my wife her dream house on the best spot in the area. Keeping the natives in line has not been easy, especially because they refuse to play by the rules. They were told over ten years ago that this land was no longer theirs, but because they were allowed to stay and fish and hunt and forage on unclaimed territory, they have forgotten their place. I've made allowances for them over the years because they have shown me and my family and the other settlers many kindnesses, and we have tried to do the same for them. However, the plain and simple fact is that the U.S. government has all along intended to relocate these people to a reservation. Why they have not done so yet eludes me. I had to fight tooth and nail to get my own land cleared before building last year, and I continue to face resistance from the Indians still living where I want to plant my gardens. Yesterday (July 22, 1888), I told California for the third time to tear down his house. He said no, sir. I was so angry that I struck him in the head, even though he was holding two infants and had a sore foot. I gave him a keg of nails and six dollars and told him to tear it down and rebuild on the beach, or he'd be sorry. Threats, violence, and money are the only things these people understand.'"

Tanya lifted her brows. "Now we're getting somewhere."

"Dan continues," Sue said. "He writes, 'Today (July 23, 1888), I told Jimmy that he must tell Taylor to take his house off my land, to take it down and put it on the beach. I told him to tell Albert the same. I gave him twelve dollars, six for Taylor and six for Albert. I don't know why I should be paying them to clear off my land. They should be paying me back rent. But it is what it is. I need to put up a barn and woodshed before the cold weather comes.'"

"He thinks he has a legitimate claim," Ellen pointed out. "In some ways, this land dispute is the fault of the government for not making things clear to either the Quileute or the settlers."

"It sounds to me like Dan was a bully," Tanya said. Turning to Ellen, she added, "You said yourself that his wife would have died in childbirth had the Quileute not helped her. He should have been more grateful."

"Listen to this," Sue continued. "'We learned today (March 8, 1889) that the president declared La Push an Indian reservation and has withdrawn it from sale and settlement; however, he said that no existing valid rights of any party shall be affected. We took this as a victory and are celebrating with friends and family at our house tonight. Hattie is happy to host guests again now that Chester has been sleeping through the night.'"

"Who's Chester?" Ellen asked.

"That's their fourth child, I think," Sue replied.

"That's interesting," Tanya mused. "The land ownership still sounds unclear, doesn't it?"

"Yes," Ellen agreed. "And I think this is about the time Dan sets fire to the village. Does he say anything about that?"

Sue skimmed over another couple of pages before saying, "He doesn't say anything explicitly about the fire, but here he says, 'If the government will not help me to defend what is rightfully mine, I will have no choice but to take matters into my own hands.'"

"That sounds pretty clear to me," Tanya insisted. "He's guilty."

"Oh, wait," Sue began. "This sounds interesting. Listen: 'I was sorry to hear that old man Howeattle, unable to accompany the tribe on their annual hops-picking trip last summer, was killed in the fire that burned down his village. I had assumed no one had remained behind. This is sad news, indeed, and my heart is troubled.'"

"That's telling," Ellen said with a nod. "He had just discovered that he was a murderer."

Sue continued, "Here, Dan writes, 'The new agent by the name of McGlinn has come today (September 14, 1889) to help the Quileute to rebuild their village and has agreed to do so on the beach. He came to the trading post to talk to me and said he wanted me to understand that until the courts decide on land ownership that the area was jointly owned by me and the tribe. If he would have stopped talking at that point, all would have ended well, but alas, he did not. He said that I should remember that the Quileute had perhaps the better claim because their forefathers held possession of the area long before I or my forefathers came over the Atlantic. I told him that I had followed the letter of the law in staking my claim and that it wasn't my fault if the law was unclear to the natives. When I asked about the rent money for the school, the agent refused to give it to me on the grounds that the land wasn't yet mine. I waited until dusk, and then I rode over and tore the school building down. Wesley won't be pleased, but the statement needed to be made.'"

"He's lost it, alright," Tanya said.

"There's one page left in this journal," Sue reported. "I'll just read this part, because it's relevant: 'The Local Land Office finally held the hearing, and I would have won if that jerk McGlinn hadn't spoken against me. He hasn't been here long enough to know the truth and has sided with the Quileute. Well, I won't stand for it and am putting in my appeal.' Then further down at the bottom of the page, he writes, 'September 4, 1891, at long last, the Local Land Office ordered that my claim entries be approved for patent. The battle is over, and we have won. We will begin the improvements to the house immediately, for Hattie wants to take in more guests. I've promised to raise the roof on the northern side and build a two-story square tower crowned with a railed widow's walk, like one we saw last summer in Seattle after visiting Baby at the zoo.'"

Sue closed the journal. "So, he got away with murder and got to keep the house."

Tanya shook her head. "But we know, in the end, he was evicted."

"There's still one journal left," Ellen pointed out.

"Can we take a break?" Tanya stood up from her chair and lifted her arms over her head. "Let's go for another walk. I need to stretch my legs."

"Sounds good," Ellen said. "I'm sure Moseby would like that, wouldn't you, boy?"

"I guess I'll join if we don't go too far," Sue said.

"Are you coming back, then?" Mary asked from behind her wide desk.

"Yes," Ellen replied. "We won't be long."

As Ellen followed her friends from the library with Moseby in his cloth pooch carrier, she had a feeling that Mary wasn't happy with them anymore and wasn't looking forward to their return.

CHAPTER FIFTEEN

The Fall of Dan Pullen

Ellen put Moseby on his leash, and then the three friends strolled outside in the cool breeze beneath a surprisingly sunny sky from the library toward River's Edge Restaurant.

Sue stopped at a bench in front of the restaurant. "I think I'll order our rental car while you guys take your walk."

"Are you sure you don't want to join us?" Tanya asked. "We aren't going far—just to the beach and back."

Sue sat on the bench and took her phone from her purse. "My feet are bothering me again. Y'all go on without me. I can see the ocean and the river from here. It's a nice spot."

Ellen and Moseby followed Tanya down the hill toward the sea. The descent wasn't as steep here as it was behind the bungalow, but without wooden steps, it was more difficult to navigate, especially with large boulders and driftwood blocking the path. Although Ellen's muscles were sore and stiff, she knew exercising them would help loosen them up.

"I hate that we're giving up," Ellen confessed once they were on the beach and walking toward the enormous driftwood—the dinosaur bones.

"We still helped, though, didn't we? By discovering that the grave was empty?"

"Yes, I suppose so."

In the distance, seals were sunning on a massive rock.

"Oh, look!" Ellen pointed.

"They're so close! Oh! He looked at me! Don't you think he's looking at me?"

"Yes!" Ellen waved. "Hi there!"

Tanya waved, too.

Moseby noticed and began to bark and wag his tail.

"Come on, Mo," Ellen said, leading him further down the beach. "You're going to scare them off."

Tanya chuckled as she followed Ellen. "I doubt little Moseby can scare them."

"Did you hear that, Mo? She's doubting you."

The friends laughed.

"He looks offended," Ellen snickered.

Tanya chuckled again. "I'm sorry, Moseby. I didn't mean to offend you."

"I wish we didn't have to leave," Ellen said after a beat.

"It's so beautiful here," Tanya agreed.

"What if Moseby and I stayed behind?"

Tanya stopped and squared herself to Ellen. "Are you serious? It's too dangerous. We were nearly killed."

Ellen shrugged. "I guess you're right. Did you hear anything about the man with the cigarette?"

"I just know he'll make it. That's all I heard."

They continued walking along the massive, petrified driftwood, stopping only when Moseby wanted to pee on it.

"Besides," Tanya said, "the tribe can take it from here. They have a plan, right?"

"I guess so."

When they reached the end of the driftwood, Ellen gazed up at the enchanted bungalow on the hill just south of where they stood.

"I hate to leave things as they are," Ellen lamented.

"We can't solve every case."

"I guess not."

They turned back and walked in silence for a few more minutes before Tanya added, "If I didn't think the tribe could handle it, I'd stay."

Ellen lifted her brows and studied Tanya. "You would?"

"Of course. I want closure as much as you do. I want the tribe to get relief from the vengeful ghost and for the ghost to find peace. You know I want those things."

"Maybe we could help the tribe. They can't break the law. They can't put their reservation in jeopardy. But we can, if necessary. Break the law, that is."

"I don't like breaking the law."

"Me either. I just mean if necessary."

"I think we should stick to the plan and go to Seattle tonight. Maybe we can find something fun to do there until we fly out on Saturday. I could use that massage you promised me. Don't you think that's best?"

Ellen sighed. "I don't know."

Ellen had gotten her hopes up, and now they were deflated again. Tears welled in her eyes, and she brushed them away. She hated leaving like this, with so much unresolved.

They walked the rest of the way in silence, until the seals came into view again. Tanya stopped to wave to them and to say goodbye. Ellen watched but didn't wave, didn't speak. She was trying not to cry.

Back at the library, Ellen gave Moseby a drink of water before returning him to his cloth pooch carrier and joining her friends at the conference table, where Sue had already begun skimming the fourth journal.

"I'm searching for something," Sue explained. "Hold on. Okay, here we go. He writes that 'the decision of the Local Land Office to accept our claims has been challenged by a land agent by the name of Carson, who has convinced the Office of Indian Affairs that I could not have lived on both the Quillayute Prairie and the La Push homesteads at the same time and therefore has accused me of deceptive practices. I have hired an attorney to take this matter back to the courts.'"

"We knew this was coming," Tanya said with a shrug.

"Oh, wow," Sue murmured.

"What?" Ellen asked impatiently.

"Dan writes, 'This evening, August 9, 1892, a gentleman appeared on my doorstep and handed over a document. It seems Hattie and I have been accused of converting to our own use monies from Baxter Fur Company over a six-year period in the amount of $18,704.51, a figure I cannot in my wildest imagination fathom to guess how it was settled upon, except that perhaps Baxter means to make it appear more credible in how precise it is. While it's true that Hattie and I have often paid for items after we'd taken them, I would venture to guess that we overpaid more often than we underpaid, and we always recorded every single one of our transactions, so this will be easy enough to disprove in court. Nevertheless, the timing couldn't be more unfortunate, given that I have already retained a lawyer to help us with the land contest.'"

"Do you think he's lying about never stealing?" Tanya wondered aloud.

"I don't know what I think about that," Sue admitted. "Let's see what else he says, and then maybe we can figure out what really happened."

Sue continued skimming the pages until she stopped and said, "Holy cow. Dan writes that until the case with Baxter was settled, all his and Hattie's personal property was confiscated—their cows, horses, chickens, wagons, a plow—enough to cover the alleged debt."

"What happened to innocent until proven guilty?" Ellen protested. "That doesn't seem fair."

"Unless they were guilty," Tanya said with a shrug.

"It says the case didn't go to trial for nearly a year," Sue continued. "Dan lost his job at the trading post and the post office. How did they make ends meet without all their farming and ranching assets, I wonder?"

"Karma is a bitch," Tanya said.

Sue crinkled her nose. "Apparently so. They started selling off land to pay their attorney and court fees. He's full of resentment in this passage, where he says he worked for Baxter seven days a week, often until midnight, and was 'drove plumb to death.' Dan writes that Baxter was sore because Dan had once mentioned he might sell him the La Push land on the hill, where Dan built Hattie's house. Dan thinks that Baxter 'saw a vein open and went for the kill,' meaning Dan was vulnerable because of the land dispute with the Quileute. Dan says, 'Baxter means to drive me to bankruptcy so he can take my castle. Well, it's Hattie's castle, and I won't let him.'"

"So, Dan was defending his home on two fronts at the same time," Ellen said.

"Oh," Sue said. "Listen to this: 'Baxter has found dozens of people—white and Quileute alike—to sign affidavits and to testify against me and Hattie and our character, implying that we must be thieves because our salaries couldn't possibly allow us to afford the lives we live. They're all lies. We work hard and have multiple sources of income. We board guests, manage the post office, rent land and farming equipment, and sell the crops we harvest and the cattle we take to slaughter. Hattie didn't steal her riding hat. She had it custom-made and delivered with Baxter's order to the trading post, but it was paid for separately, and we have the receipt to prove it. I also have the receipts for the materials I purchased to build our house. As for the governess, she began as a person in our employment, but once we opened a room in our house to be a school for the children of settlers, the school district paid her as a public-school teacher for much of the year and we paid her for the rest. Lies are being told about us in the court by people who hate us because we have more than they. But today, Baxter crossed a line when he testified that I was honest until I married. He's making it look like Hattie has manipulated me into stealing for her. I can't let him get away with that.'"

"So how did it end?" Tanya asked.

"Yeah, Sue. Get to the juicy part," Ellen teased.

"Apparently Baxter's case fell apart," Sue said as she skimmed over the next page. "Looks like he paid most of the people to testify against the Pullens. And a team of accountants tasked by the court with assessing the books found that they were kept honestly. The jury found the defendants innocent on June 26, 1893."

"Well, I hope that was the right verdict," Tanya said.

"Dan writes that Baxter didn't give up," Sue said. "He took them to court two more times. But it looks like Dan did the same thing with his land dispute. When an Indian agent demanded that they vacate their home within sixty days, the Pullens filed for a restraining order against him. Gosh, it looks like Dan and Hattie spent years in court with one or the other case. They turned their house on the hill into a seaside resort to help make ends meet. Let's see, it says here that in the summer of 1896, Dan left to find work in Seattle to offset their court costs, but a newspaper article speculated that Dan's disappearance from La Push mean that he'd offed himself. Dan writes, 'That reporter has no idea how close he came to reporting the truth. We are so far in debt, that for the first time I fear we may lose the house even if we win the land contest.'"

"That's sad," Ellen sympathized. "I don't care what he did, when someone contemplates suicide, it's sad."

Mary had gone to the back room to have her lunch but returned just as Ellen had made her comment. As usual, the librarian's poker face gave nothing away.

"No, I agree," Sue said. "But it gets worse."

"Worse than suicide?" Tanya asked.

"The next summer, the summer of 1897, Hattie showed up to Dan's logging camp at Port Gamble with their sons, Dee and Royal. She'd left their youngest, Chester, with Dan's sister, Sarah, and had enrolled Mildred in the state boarding school, Ellensburg Normal. Oh, you didn't know there was a school named for you, did you, Ellen?"

"No, I didn't." Ellen chuckled. "So, what happened?"

"When Hattie arrived, she told Dan she was bound for Alaska to start a new life. Her brother David's widow, Annie, would run their boarding house in La Push for as long as the house was theirs. He writes, 'I couldn't believe that, after all we'd been through, she was giving up. I tried to convince her that we would win the house and the land and that everything would go back to the way it was, but she refused to listen. She said it was over and that I needed to face the truth. She said she would send for the boys once she was settled. I reached down to kiss her, and she gave me her cheek. She's turned cold and hard against me, as though I'm the cause of all her woes, when, truth be told, I have been the one fighting tooth and nail to save her castle and our family. Let her go, ungrateful tramp. I know what she's really after.'"

"What do you think he means by that?" Ellen wondered. "Does he suspect her of having an affair?"

"That's what it sounds like," Tanya said. "Does it say anything more about that?"

"Let me see." Sue skimmed the next page. "Oh, this is sad. He writes that Dee, at age twelve, had the job of oiling the skid roads to help the logs move faster, and Royal, at age ten, had to clean out the stables and help the cook in the kitchen. I guess they didn't get to go to school anymore."

"That is sad," Tanya agreed.

"Skid roads?" Ellen repeated. "That's the origin of skid row. Dan went from being the king of his castle to living at the bottom of the barrel."

"What does he say about Hattie?" Tanya asked.

"Oh, here we go. He writes, 'After hearing rumors that my wife refers to herself as a widow, I decided to accompany our sons on the voyage to Skagway to make the truth known. Although my hearing has worsened and my strength isn't what it once was, I am not, in fact, dead. I discovered Hattie had claimed an abandoned waterfront cabin, where she sleeps in a cot hanging from the ceiling. She intends for our sons to sleep on beds of hay. I insisted on staying to improve their living conditions by building a two-story house with rooms for the rest of our family and my sister Sarah. Hattie has sent for her horses and plans to haul supplies for the miners coming for the Klondike gold. She's resourceful, my Hattie, but she is clearly no longer my Hattie, and as soon as she and the children are settled, I plan to return to the logging camp.'"

"His words are full of innuendo," Ellen started, "but he makes no direct accusations."

"It says here," Sue continued, "that in July of 1998, the Pullens were notified by a judge that their case against the Indian agent had been dismissed but that if Dan wished to bring charges against the Chief of the Indian Bureau and the Secretary of the Interior, to kindly inform him, as there had been other suits filed against them. Dan writes, 'Our lawyer refuses to work with me because I owe him money, so I wrote to the judge to inform him that I will have to hire another attorney. I told the judge I would notify him when I was ready, but I wrote that letter to retain my reputation. I am done. I was doing it all for Hattie, and she is no longer my Hattie, so what is there worth fighting for? I am broken and alone and without a nickel to my name. I don't care much what becomes of me. I only wish to one day return to my idyllic prairie at Quillayute, even if it's only in a box in the ground.'"

"He should have been in that grave," Ellen said. "It's what he wanted."

"That's probably why he's so vengeful," Sue pointed out.

Tanya sighed. "I hope the tribe can convince his family to put him where he belongs."

CHAPTER SIXTEEN

The Enchanted Bungalow

Sitting beside Moseby in the back seat of the new rental—another white Nissan Rogue—Ellen couldn't stop her hands from trembling or her teeth from chattering as Sue drove up the hill toward the enchanted bungalow. Tanya, in the passenger's seat, glanced nervously at Ellen while Sue put the vehicle in park. They sat there in silence for a long moment, staring at the house. Dread filled Ellen's heart as she tried to muster up the courage to go inside.

"Let's get this over with," Sue finally said.

Tanya unhooked her safety harness. "Stick to the plan, okay?"

Ellen and Sue nodded.

"In and out," Tanya stated. "Nothing more."

"You don't have to worry about me," Sue said.

Ellen took a deep breath. "Or me."

After the Chevy Traverse had exploded, Officer Pullen had driven them by the house to pick up their purses and a change of clothes for Sue, who had still been wearing her pajamas. They'd had to dart past flying silverware and struggle with slamming doors, but they'd managed to get out unscathed. This time, however, they would need more time to grab their bags and Ellen's equipment. As tempted as Ellen was to leave her paranormal devices behind, some of them had been hard to find and wouldn't be easy to replace.

Ellen kissed Mo before leaving him in the back seat, along with her purse. The only thing she took with her was the key to the house, which she had tucked in her pants' pocket. Sue and Tanya, also empty-handed, followed her onto the porch. They took nothing that would impede them from grabbing as many things as they could.

"Here we go." Ellen turned the key in the lock and opened the door.

They were immediately alarmed by the arrangement of the furniture. The couch, chair, and floor lamp had been moved up against one another in the center of the room, as if someone were preparing the room to be painted. Silverware lay strewn across the floor. The small vase of flowers that Sue had bought for Tanya lay on its side, and water was dripping from the kitchen counter to the living-room floor.

"What's that?" Tanya pointed to something on the big, picture window on the opposite side of the house.

"It looks like blood," Sue said with a shaky voice.

Ellen cautiously crossed the room to take a closer look. It *was* blood. Splotches of it spotted the window in seven different places. As she glanced on the porch outside, she jumped back and gasped. Seven seagulls lay dead with their beaks smashed in.

Her friends caught up to her.

Tanya covered her mouth and backed away.

"Oh, my gawd," Sue whispered. "Let's hurry and get the hell out of here."

Just then, another seagull flew right into the glass with a horrible thud—an eerily savage sound—and dropped to the ground. It writhed for a moment and then lay still.

"In and out," Tanya reminded them. "Grab your stuff in one trip."

Sue, who stood between them, glanced first at Ellen and then at Tanya. "Ready?"

The friends nodded and took off running for their respective rooms. The silverware sprang into action. Ellen held her hands in front of her face as she dashed up the stairs to the loft. She was worried more for Sue, who wasn't very fast, than for herself. The force with which the utensils flew across the room was powerful enough to lodge a fork or knife into their bodies, as it had been the first night when a fork had pierced the front door.

Most of her things were still in her overnight bag. Anything else would be left behind. She zipped up the medium-sized case and, pulling it by the handle, dragged it behind her as she returned downstairs, where she had expected to find Tanya and Sue.

Had they beaten her out to the car?

Then she heard water running in the bathroom. What had happened to their plan of in and out?

"Tanya?" Ellen called as she poked her head into the bathroom doorway.

Steam filled the room, but it wasn't too thick to prevent Ellen from seeing the writing on the mirror over the sink: *You broke your promise.*

"A week isn't up," Ellen murmured. "I haven't broken it yet. You broke it by trying to kill Sue."

A knife pierced through the back of her thigh, up high near her behind, before it fell to the floor, but not without gouging her and drawing blood.

"Stop," Ellen shouted at the ghost of Dan Pullen. "Enough!"

But the silverware continued to fly.

"Ellen?" Tanya's voice carried through the house, along with the sound of banging against the door. "My door won't open! The French doors either! I'm trapped! Ellen? Help!"

"Tanya?" Sue's voice carried from the front bedroom. "I'm trapped, too! Ellen? Are you there?"

"I'm here!" Ellen shouted, as she ran past the silverware to Tanya's bedroom door. She turned the knob, which wasn't locked, but when she pushed against the door, it wouldn't budge. "Don't worry! I'll get you out of here."

Ellen rushed to Sue's door, dodging silverware, but was faced with the same problem.

"Call 9-1-1!" Sue cried. "My phone is out of service!"

"I didn't bring mine!" Tanya bemoaned.

Ellen had left hers behind, too. She'd never managed to get service in the bungalow, so she hadn't seen any reason to bring it.

"I'm getting you out! I promise!"

Ellen thought it might be easier to break them out from the outside, by throwing one of the heavy chairs through a window. With this plan in mind, she dragged her case to the front door and turned the knob. But that door, too, wouldn't budge. Using her key did no good. The door wouldn't move.

A fork flew at her and scratched the skin of her forearm.

"Stop!" she cried again. "Let us go! We'll leave you in peace!" But the door still wouldn't budge as she pulled at it with all her might.

Leaving her case near the front door, she ran through the flying silverware to the kitchen door, but it, too, would not budge. She lifted the window over the sink. It only moved a few inches before it, too, jammed.

"Help!" she screamed through the small opening in the window. "Is anyone there? Please help us!"

"Ellen?" Tanya shouted. "Are you okay?"

"I'm trapped, too!" she said. "Shout for help, in case anyone is down on the beach."

Ellen heard Tanya and Sue shouting.

"Can you open a window?" Ellen cried.

"No!" Tanya called out. "I've already tried."

"Neither can I!" Sue shouted. "Ellen, can you throw the rocking chair through the big window?"

"I'll give it a try!"

Ellen rushed from the kitchen to where the furniture was sitting in the center of the room. The rocking chair was heavy, but Ellen managed to lift it. She swung around, like she used to swing her kids by their hands. The rocking chair lifted as she swung, and after two spins, she hurled it at the window.

The chair hit the pane with a thud and fell to the ground without cracking the glass.

Ellen picked it up and tried again. And again. She was exhausted.

She shrieked when another seagull slammed into the pane from the other side, living another splotch of blood as it fell to the porch.

Angry now, she stormed to the kitchen window, and in her loudest voice, screamed, "I'm trapped in the bungalow! Please help me!"

She repeated it until her throat burned and she was sure it must be bleeding.

Then a knife flew at her from the side and cut a slash in her upper arm.

"Dan Pullen!" Ellen shouted angrily. "Stop taking your misery out on us! We weren't the ones who accused you of stealing from the company's business! We weren't the ones who tried to take your land! We didn't drive Hattie and the kids away from you! We aren't the cause of your misery! Is that Hattie's wedding silverware you're hurling at me? How do you think she'd feel if she knew you had weaponized it?"

The silverware fell to the ground.

Feeling encouraged, Ellen said, "I read your journals. I know you had some rotten luck. I know people did you wrong. I'm sorry. I'm sorry for you. Let me help you."

Using the blood splotched on the picture window, the ghost of Dan Pullen wrote: *You broke your promise.*

Ellen shook her head. "Burning down the resort is not the answer. Just like burning down the Quileute village wasn't the answer over a hundred years ago. You should have been prosecuted for that, you do realize? Aren't you responsible for Howeattle's death? Do you really want more blood on your hands?"

Another knife flew at her from the living room, coming directly for her face. What had she been thinking, talking to him like that? She covered her eyes and ducked before screaming, "Help! Can anyone hear me? I'm trapped in the bungalow!"

A pounding against the back kitchen door made her jump.

"Ellen?" a voice—a man's—called.

"Yes! Who are you?" she cried, wondering how he knew her name.

"It's Ben. I heard you screaming."

"I'm trapped. We all are. Can you use the chairs on the porch to break through the bedroom windows and get my friends out?"

"I'll try. Hold on."

Ellen saw the young man dart by the picture window toward the back bedroom.

"Stand back, Tanya!" Ellen warned as she hurried to the window to watch. "Ben is going to break through your bedroom window."

"Who's Ben?" Sue asked from the front bedroom.

Ellen shook her head, wondering why it mattered who he was. He was here to help. "A young man I met. Hold tight!"

The sound of glass shattering caused Ellen to shiver and rejoice at the same time.

Tanya appeared at the back window, where the dead seagulls lay. "I'm out! We'll get you out, too!"

"Thank goodness," Ellen whispered, realizing for the first time that her throat killed her when she tried to speak.

Moments later, all three of them were visible through the picture window. Ellen squinted at the sight of a fourth person. It was transparent and bright—the apparition of the Native American she'd seen that first day on the beach. He was standing behind Ben. Just as Ben lifted the chair to use against the big window, the front door opened wide, as if pushed open by a gust of wind.

"Wait!" Ellen shouted. "The door opened! Meet me around the front!"

Ellen grabbed the handle of her bag and dragged it through the front door. She supposed Dan had realized she was getting out one way or another, so he gave up. Or maybe the apparition of the Native American had opened the door.

"Thank you!" Ellen said to Ben as soon as she saw him again. She threw her arms around his neck. "You're a lifesaver."

The apparition was no longer behind him.

"Thank you," Ellen said again, this time to the man she had seen, in case he could still hear her. Then, turning to her friends, she asked, "Should we leave the equipment?"

Tanya glared at her. "Do you have to ask?"

"What happened?" Ben wanted to know.

"Can someone else explain?" Ellen whispered. "I shredded my vocal cords."

As they carried their bags from the front porch to the rental, where Moseby was wining, Sue explained to Ben what had transpired. Ellen was sorry to leave her good instruments behind. She hoped she could replace them.

"We're so lucky you were on the beach," Tanya said.

"The tribe asked me to keep an eye on you. That's why I've been hanging around." Ben helped them load their things into the back of the car.

"We'll have to thank them," Sue said as she opened the door to the driver's side and climbed in. "Who knows what might have become of us? You heard about the fire?"

Ben closed the hatchback. "Scary stuff. I can't believe you were brave enough to go back into the house."

"Brave or stupid," Tanya grumbled as she climbed into the passenger's side.

"You're bleeding," Ben said to Ellen.

"It's not as bad as it looks." Ellen slid into the back seat with Moseby. She took her dog into her arms. "It's okay, boy."

"What are you going to do now?" Ben asked.

"We're staying our last few nights in Seattle," Sue answered. "We fly out on Saturday."

"Do you need a ride anywhere?" Tanya offered Ben.

"Nah, I'm good. I'm just glad you guys are alright."

They thanked the young man again before closing the car doors and backing down the long driveway. Sue drove down the hill away from the enchanted bungalow. Ellen gazed at it through her car window. Tears of frustration fell on her cheeks. She brushed them away. Tanya had been right: They couldn't solve every case.

CHAPTER SEVENTEEN

Seattle

B y the time Ellen and her friends had reached Seattle, they were hungry and thirsty but too tired to dine out, so they drove through a hamburger joint and picked up food to take back with them to the hotel. On the way, Tanya had searched on her phone for a place to stay. They'd decided they wanted a two-bedroom suite instead of separate, standard rooms, because they were too shaken up to sleep alone. Tanya had booked the presidential suite at the Hyatt Regency, and Ellen couldn't wait to eat, take a hot shower, and go to bed.

She probably needed a bandage for the back of her thigh. It hadn't stopped bleeding, and she'd had to sit on a towel to protect the car seat. Although she couldn't see the back of her pants, she was sure they were ruined—not just from the hole caused by the knife, but from the blood.

"Turn that up," Sue requested from the front as they neared the sleek hotel in the middle of downtown, just past the Space Needle and Pike Place Market. "She's talking about Dan Pullen's grave."

"Really?" Tanya leaned forward and turned up the radio.

Ellen leaned forward, too, her heart picking up speed.

The voice of a female reporter was saying, "Hear the fascinating story of a grave that was found dug up and empty at nine-o'clock on *CBS News Tonight* when we talk to the great-granddaughter of the man who was supposed to be buried there."

Ellen pulled out her phone to check the time. "It's already eight-fifteen."

"And look at this line." Sue pulled behind a half-dozen cars waiting for valet parking.

Tanya gave Ellen a worried glance. "Do you think we can get checked in and into our suite in time to watch?"

"I sure hope so," Ellen said.

"Y'all get us checked in," Sue decided. "Mo and I will wait in line for the valet."

"Do you want your food?" Ellen asked.

"Just my fries." Sue took a sip of her cherry coke.

Ellen handed her the fries, and then she and Tanya climbed out with their food and drinks, took their bags from the back of the rental, and hurried into the hotel lobby. Ellen wasn't so rushed that she didn't notice the high ceilings and the gorgeous light fixtures covering every square inch of them. They looked like free-floating candles, like something from *Harry Potter*. The enormous room was industrial chic with floor to ceiling windows, glittery gold and silver accents, and tall and smooth industrial columns that dwarfed the four check-in counters and the people manning them.

A line of eight people had already formed ahead of them, but with four employees checking people in, Ellen hoped it wouldn't be a problem.

And yet, after ten minutes and no movement in the line, she began to worry.

"What's the hold up?" Ellen whispered to Tanya.

Tanya tapped on her phone. "I wonder if *CBS News* posts their stories online."

"Good idea." Ellen tucked her drink beneath her arm and took out her phone. "You look for that while I see if it's possible to check into the hotel online. It might speed up the process."

The line moved, and now there were seven in front of them.

"They don't have anything about Pullen's grave on their website," Tanya said after a while. "Maybe they'll post something once the segment airs."

"What if they don't? I'd hate to miss it." Ellen continued to search for an app that would allow her to check in.

"Excuse me, Ma'am," a young woman said from behind Ellen. "Do you know that you're bleeding?"

"It looks worse than it is," Ellen replied. "But thank you."

After a few minutes, Tanya said, "I found the online check-in and checked us in, so all we'll have to do is pick up the keys."

"Oh, you figured it out. Thank you."

The man in front of them asked, "There's a way to check in online?"

Tanya showed him how, and then showed the couple in line before him. The young woman behind them asked for help, too.

When they reached the desk, it was a quarter to nine. Soon after, they headed for the elevators. Sue entered with Mo and her luggage and caught up to them by the time the elevator doors opened.

"Moseby!" Ellen cooed in the sweet voice she only used with her dog. "Who's got you?"

"Perfect timing," Tanya said to Sue.

"Let's hope these elevators aren't as slow as molasses," Sue commented as they waited for a man to exit.

Ellen recalled their experience at the Biltmore last Christmas. "Don't jinx them."

"Seriously." Tanya entered the elevator first and pushed the button for the forty-fifth floor. "Hurry, before more people come."

Ellen and Sue boarded, and Tanya pushed the button to close the elevator doors just as a little girl in pigtails ran to get on.

"Oops." Tanya shrugged when the girl was unable to board.

"She'll live," Sue reassured Tanya.

Just when they thought they were home free, the elevator stopped for a group on the second floor, which was apparently where the hotel bar was located. The ride up seemed to take forever as they stopped on numerous floors, where people got off and on, off and on. Ellen glanced at the time on her phone every few seconds. It was a few minutes past nine when they finally reached their floor.

"I'll bring your bag." Ellen turned to Tanya. "You run!"

Tanya fled down the hall with the keys and her drink. Ellen and Sue hurried after her. Fortunately, there were only a few suites on the top floor, and they quickly reached theirs.

Cool grays, earth tones, and a touch of teal greeted them as Ellen and Sue entered the suite, where Tanya had already turned on the television in the living room and was scouring the guide for the CBS channel.

"Come here, Moseby-Mo," Ellen said as she took her dog from Sue and removed him from his cloth pooch carrier. "Thank you, Sue."

Ellen put Mo down and went to the bathroom to look at the back of her pants. The upper part of the pant leg was stained with dried blood. Carefully, she removed the pants to inspect her wound. Although it wasn't wide, it was deeper than she'd thought and might need stitches.

"Found it," Tanya said.

Ellen quickly washed the back of her leg and wrapped a towel around her waist before rejoining her friends in front of the television. Moseby followed her.

The three friends sat on the sleek, gray sectional eating their burgers while they waited for the anchors to get to their segment on Dan Pullen's grave. Ellen fed Moseby some of her fries.

Fifteen minutes into the broadcast, Sue announced, "This is it."

A female correspondent stood opposite a woman in her seventies. The woman had short, curly, red and white hair and intense, blue eyes.

"I'm standing here with Nora Phillips, the great-granddaughter of a man whose grave was found dug up and empty at Quillayute Prairie Cemetery early yesterday morning. Police have no known suspects in the case. Nora, thank you for talking with us tonight. First, do you have any idea who might have vandalized your great-grandfather's grave?"

"No idea. He was never buried there. Everyone in the family knows it."

"That's interesting, Nora, but why have an empty grave? Or was it empty? Could the vandals have been after something?"

Nora smiled nervously. "My mother explained it like this. Her father, who was Daniel Pullen's oldest son, also named Daniel but called Dee, wanted to cremate his father so he could carry him with him back here to Seattle. Of the four children, Dee was the closest to his father, so I guess he got his way, but his father had already paid for a plot, casket, and headstone. So, his family buried the casket with a few personal gifts from family members. My grandfather put in a baseball. My great uncle Royal added a handkerchief his mother had embroidered. Supposedly, my great uncle Chester laid his father's rifle in there. I can't imagine anyone digging up the grave for it, but who knows?"

"And where are Daniel Pullen's ashes now?"

"After my mother passed, they were handed down to me. I have them in a bronze urn on a mantle in my basement beside the ashes of my mother."

Ellen and her friends exchanged looks of excitement.

"I wonder how open Nora would be to spreading his ashes on his grave," Sue said.

"I suppose when I pass," Nora continued, "their ashes—and mine—will go to my daughter in Chicago, since my husband preceded me in death two years ago."

"Guys, we have to pay her a visit while we're here," Ellen insisted. "We can't leave without trying."

"Agreed," Sue said.

Ellen and Sue glanced at Tanya, who shrugged and said, "I'm in."

Early the next morning, after taking Mo for a walk around the hotel, Ellen left her dog with her friends to have her wound cleaned, stitched, and bandaged at an emergency clinic. It took a few hours, and by the time she'd returned to their hotel suite, her friends had fresh croissants and coffee waiting for her, had found the address and phone number of Nora Phillips, and had arranged to meet with Nora later that afternoon.

Ellen took a sip of hot coffee. It felt good on her sore throat—still hoarse from screaming.

"What should we do until then?" Tanya asked. "Massages?"

"Definitely," Ellen said. "And they're on me."

Rejuvenated from massages and delicious salads at the hotel, the three friends, along with Moseby, took the Nissan Rogue to their four o'clock appointment to meet Dan Pullen's great-granddaughter. Nora Phillips lived in a Seattle suburb called Bothell about thirty minutes away from downtown.

The gray and white, two-story, split-level home sat on a large, tree-lined lot with a wooden privacy fence running the length of the right side, all the way to the curb. Next to the privacy fence was a wide drive-way that led to a two-car garage. From the driveaway, stone steps cut through flower beds uphill toward the upper-level entry to a set of double wooden doors, painted darker gray than the cedar siding on the house. To Ellen, it seemed as if everything was gray these days. Although there was no fence in the front yard on the left side of the property, a line of fir trees hid the house next door.

Ellen tucked Moseby into his cloth pooch carrier and followed Sue and Tanya from the curb, down the driveaway, and up the steps to the front doors. Sue rang the bell.

Moments later, Nora appeared wearing a wide smile. "Hello. What? No camera crew?"

"Oh, we're not reporters," Sue explained.

"No?" Nora's eyes widened. "I thought you wanted to interview me about my great-grandfather's grave?"

"Yes, but we aren't reporters," Ellen said. "We're paranormal investigators."

Nora blinked; her smile faded.

"May we come in?" Sue asked.

Nora rolled her eyes. "I should have known people like you would come out of the woodwork after last night's interview. I'm sorry, but I'm not interested."

Nora was about to close the door when Sue put her foot on the threshold. "Don't you want to hear what we have to say? We've read your great-grandfather's journals. We know he wanted to be buried on the Quillayute Prairie."

"Why is that any business of yours?" Nora demanded. "It's for his family to decide."

"You don't care about his wishes?" Tanya pressed. "What if his spirit is restless because they weren't honored?"

"That's a cruel thing to say." Nora glanced down at Sue's foot and then glared at her. "Do you mind?"

Sue removed her foot, and the door was slammed shut.

The three friends exchanged worried glances.

"Now what do we do?" Tanya wondered out loud.

Ellen sighed. She'd been so sure that this was going to be the key to finding closure to this case. Turning back toward the car, she noted, "Maybe Mary Pullen will have better luck. Let's send her Nora's contact info."

As Ellen removed Mo from his cloth pooch carrier and put him in the back seat of the Rogue, he barked at a black cat that had appeared in the lawn. The cat darted around the left side of the lot, toward the row of fir trees, and disappeared into the house through a small, basement window.

That gave Ellen an idea.

CHAPTER EIGHTEEN

Priestess Isabel

N o way," Tanya argued during the drive back to the Hyatt Regency, after Ellen had shared her idea. "We're not stealing a dead man's ashes. That's just wrong."

Ellen wanted to say that they couldn't very well steal a *living* man's ashes, but she held her tongue, saving the joke for another time.

"Just think about it," Sue persuaded. "We wouldn't really be stealing. We'd be putting them where they belong."

Tanya shook her head. "Not against the family's wishes."

"But is it really the family's wishes to keep the ashes with Nora?" Ellen asked. "It sounds like the other relatives wanted him buried at the prairie."

"But you don't have their permission," Tanya pointed out. "The decision rests with the family."

"Aren't Dan's wishes what matter most?" Sue challenged.

Tanya gave an exasperated sigh. "Quit ganging up on me. If you want to do it, do it. Just count me out."

Ellen frowned. The size of the basement window had been small—too narrow for Ellen or Sue to fit through. "We can't do it without you."

"No way. It's not fair that it's always me. I'm not doing it."

"I have an idea," Sue said. "Don't you have Priestess Isabel on a retainer? Why don't we ask her to throw the bones?"

"I didn't know that," Ellen said. "How much do you pay her?"

They had met and consulted with the Voodoo priestess during a case in New Orleans involving Delphine LaLaurie, Marie Laveau, and the devil child of Bourbon Street.

"Two hundred a month," Sue disclosed. "Isn't that right, Tanya?"

"Yes. I call her at least twice a month, sometimes more."

"I should do that, too," Ellen said. "Why have you never told me this?"

"I thought you knew," Sue said.

"I'm sure I told you," Tanya insisted. "Maybe you weren't paying attention."

Ellen blanched and had been about to defend herself when she bit her tongue. She needed Tanya on her side.

"Will you do it?" Sue asked Tanya. "Will you ask Priestess Isabel what we should do?"

Tanya thought about it for a few moments and finally said, "Okay. Fine. But if she says no, you guys have to back off."

"And if she says yes, you're in, right?" Ellen asked.

"I guess so."

"Why don't we stop somewhere for a snack and call her from there?" Sue suggested. "I'm craving something sweet."

"Won't we spoil our dinner?" Ellen asked.

"I didn't think we'd be eating another meal after that late lunch," Sue said.

Ellen laughed. "Since when have we ever skipped a meal?"

"I'm hungry for something sweet, too," Tanya said.

"Then something sweet it is," Ellen declared. "Let the birthday girl choose."

"Tanya's birthday was over several days ago," Sue complained. "I don't know why she gets to pick."

"Because I'm the one who needs convincing," Tanya said. "And right now, I want an ice cream sundae with strawberries and almonds sprinkled on top."

"Could you be any more specific?" Sue teased.

"I'm Googling ice cream parlors now," Ellen said from the back. "There's a Baskin-Robbins only five minutes away."

They picked up ice cream to go, and, since Ellen got a single mint chocolate chip scoop on a cone and could eat and drive, she got behind the wheel while Sue took her spot with a sundae in the back seat with Moseby. Then, once they were on the highway back to Seattle, Tanya called Priestess Isabel and put her on speaker.

"Hello there, Miss Tanya," the Voodoo priestess said. "I had a feelin' I'd hear from you soon. Can you call me back in about thirty minutes? I just sat down to my dinner."

"Absolutely," Tanya said. "We'll talk then."

The three friends sat on the balcony of their hotel suite overlooking Elliott Bay, where the sun was beginning to set, and a light smattering of rain caused the water to dance and twinkle in the waning light.

They had blankets and mugs of warm coffee, something Ellen couldn't imagine them doing in Texas in May. What a nice break from the heat this trip had been if nothing else. Ellen vowed that she would make more frequent trips in the spring and summers to Portland with Brian when he travelled there for business or to visit his brother's family.

"It's been thirty minutes," Sue told Tanya.

"I'm calling her now."

Ellen cuddled Mo in her lap, making sure he was warm. He'd been such a good boy, so easy to travel with, and a comfort when she was scared. Maybe she'd take him on more trips with her in the future.

"Hello, Miss Tanya," Priestess Isabel said over the speaker on Tanya's phone. "I'm ready to throw the bones for you. What's your question?"

"I'm not sure how to phrase it. I read the journal of a deceased man who wanted to be buried at a prairie, but his great-granddaughter has his ashes at home and doesn't seem to care. I want you to ask the bones if my friends and I should steal the ashes and put them where they are meant to be, or if we should mind our own business."

"You're asking me if you should break the law?" the Voodoo priestess asked. "That sounds familiar."

Ellen stifled a giggle. "Hello, Priestess Isabel. This is Ellen."

"And Sue."

"Hello, my friends. How are you?"

"Confused," Sue said. "That's why we're talking to you."

"We were attacked by the man's vengeful ghost," Tanya explained. "We know he's not at peace."

"Okay. I'm shaking the bones."

They heard a series of thuds and clatters over the phone before Isabel began, "This is interesting, Miss Tanya. Knowing you, I don't think this is what you want to hear. The bones indicate a severe lack of harmony that needs fixin'. Only by righting a past wrong can this harmony be restored. It seems to me that the bones are clear about the ashes being returned to the grave. But let me give them another shake to see if breaking the law is the right path, or if God wants you to go in another direction."

"Okay," Tanya said in a worried tone.

The sequence of thuds and clatters came over the speaker of Tanya's phone once more. Priestess Isabel could be heard saying, "Uh-huh. Well, hmm. Okay."

Ellen resisted the urge to ask questions.

"So, Miss Tanya, this is what I see. The bone that represents *obstacles* is in the center of my mat. My shell representing *attack* is touching it, as is the red button that means *action*. This seems clear to me that the bones want you to attack your obstacles with action, even if it means breaking the law."

Ellen couldn't stop the smile from spreading across her face. Sue was grinning, too. Tanya gnawed on her lower lip.

"Are you sure?" Tanya asked.

"The bone that means *body* landed on the place in my mat that represents the distant past. The bones have spoken, Miss Tanya, whether you like what they have to say or not."

"Okay, Priestess," Tanya said. "Thank you so much for your time. I'll call you again soon. Have a good night."

"You ladies take care," Isabel said. "Be careful, and please send me a text and let me know how it all turns out."

"Will do," Ellen promised.

"Bye," Sue said.

"Goodbye," Isabel echoed.

Tanya ended the call and eyed her friends. "So, what's the plan?"

"We have to get Nora away from her house," Ellen stated. "I'll call her and pretend to be a reporter wanting to meet her at a restaurant in downtown Seattle. While she's away, we go in—"

"You mean *I* go in," Tanya corrected.

"Tanya goes in and pours Dan's ashes into my tote. We'll replace the ashes with dirt or something—oh, maybe some gray grout—so she never knows the difference. Then we'll take his ashes back to the Quillayute Prairie Cemetery and sprinkle them over his grave."

"Sounds like a plan," Sue said. "Tanya?"

"Are we sure she lives alone?" Tanya asked.

"Her husband died and her daughter lives in Chicago," Sue said. "I suppose she might have a roommate, but it seems unlikely."

"When I call to invite her for dinner," Ellen began, "I'll tell her she's welcome to bring any family or friends who might be living with her."

Tanya rolled her eyes. "Okay. Let's do it."

<u>CHAPTER NINETEEN</u>

Thieves in the Night

Ellen sat in the back seat of the Nissan Rogue—she'd left Mo at the hotel—and watched Nora's house from across the street, two houses down. The rain was falling heavier than it had been earlier that evening when they'd watched the sunset from their balcony and had listened to Priestess Isabel's reading. Ellen hadn't anticipated the streetlamp in front of Nora's house and the bright circle of light she and her friends must cross until they reached the row of fir trees. She hoped and prayed none of the neighbors were watching.

"I hope this rain lets up," Sue said from behind the wheel. "Though I guess it might make us harder to spot by the neighbors."

When one of the garage doors began to open, Ellen's heart began to race.

"Is that her leaving?" Tanya asked from the passenger's seat.

A blue SUV—a Honda Pilot—backed out of the drive and paused near the curb while the garage door closed. Then it drove off in the direction Ellen and her friends had come—toward an Italian restaurant called The Pink Door in downtown Seattle for the meeting that would never take place.

"Better hurry," Ellen urged once Nora and her car were out of sight.

Ellen carried an empty tote and a plastic container filled with gray, powdery grout from Home Depot as she followed Tanya down the dark street toward the gray, two-story, split-level home they intended to burglarize tonight. Sue followed with a flashlight, which she had yet to turn on, so as not to alert the neighbors. This entire plan hinged on the hope that the basement window would still be open for what they had assumed was Nora's black cat.

But with the heavy rain, Ellen wasn't feeling optimistic.

They made their way to the left side of the house, near the row of firs, where Sue turned on the flashlight to help guide them toward the house. Ellen held her breath until the small basement window came into view.

"It's closed," Tanya said. "Sorry, guys."

"Wait." Sue moved closer to the house. "That's a cat door. Can you see the hinges? The window pushes in and out."

Ellen crouched near the window, blinking the rain out of her eyes. They hadn't carried umbrellas because they were trying to be inconspicuous, but they were getting drenched.

As Ellen pushed against the windowpane, it gave. She pushed it as far as it would go and looked inside. A lamp was turned on. It sat on an end table beside a sofa where the black cat was licking itself. It looked up at Ellen and hissed.

"It's okay, kitty," Ellen said sweetly.

Tanya crouched beside Ellen. "I'm not sure I can fit through that opening."

"Sure, you can," Ellen encouraged. "Just go in feet first with your arms over your head."

Tanya gave her a wry grin. "Sounds easy."

"If anyone can do it, you can," Sue said.

"Yeah, right," Tanya said. "Lying won't help anything. Can you see if there's something beneath the window? Something I could hurt myself on when landing?"

Ellen pressed her head through the opening. The cat hissed at her again. "There's a couch. Oh, perfect! Just fall on your bottom on the couch. Easy peasy. That's probably what the cat does."

"And we all know I have the dexterity of a cat," Tanya said dryly.

As Sue held the light, Tanya sat on the wet ground, slid her legs through the opening, and scooted forward on her bottom, until her hips were through. Then she carefully eased in until she was hanging by her arms from the window ledge.

"I can almost reach the back of the couch," Tanya said. "I can feel it with the tip of my toes."

"Just let yourself go," Ellen coached. "It'll be a soft landing."

"Here goes nothing."

Tanya let go of the window and cried. "Oh!"

Ellen pushed her head through the opening. "Are you okay?"

Tanya looked up at her from where she sat on the sofa. "I'm fine. It just scared me, that's all. Drop down the empty tote."

Ellen dropped the tote, but when she heard Tanya cry, "Oh, no!" she poked her head through the door again.

"What's wrong?" Ellen asked.

"The urns. They're both bronze!"

Ellen studied them from where she was crouched at the window, her head still poking in through the cat door. "The one on the right is more of a shiny brass, isn't it? Pick them up and see if there's anything inscribed on them."

Tanya handled the urns, inspecting them from top to bottom. "There's nothing inscribed. Nothing at all. What do we do?"

"Does one look older than the other?" Sue asked from behind Ellen.

"The darker one looks older. Ellen's right about the one on the right looking more like shiny brass than bronze."

"Then go with the one on the left," Ellen said. "We've gone this far. We may as well take a chance."

"And what if it's the wrong one?" Tanya asked anxiously. "What if we accidentally spread Nora's mother's ashes instead of Dan's?"

"Should we take both ashes, just in case?" Sue wondered.

"Absolutely not," Tanya said. "Dan wants to rest on the prairie, but we don't know Nora's mother's wishes."

Ellen shook her head. "The one on the left is clearly bronze, Tanya. Please, just empty those ashes into the tote, and let's get out of here."

Headlights appeared on the street. Sue killed her light. Ellen held her breath. When the car finally passed, Ellen took in a deep gulp of air.

Through the window, Ellen watched Tanya lift the lid of the bronze urn and pour the ashes into the tote. Specks of the dust whirled up in the air and into Tanya's face—bits of Dan Pullen flying through the room. Then Tanya opened the plastic grout container and poured some of it into the urn. She didn't need the whole container to equal what she had taken in ash. Then she returned the urn to the mantle and carried the tote of ashes to the window. She climbed up on the back of the couch and handed the tote to Ellen, who passed it back to Sue. Then she passed up the container with the rest of the grout.

"Give me your hand, Ellen," Tanya said from where she stood on the back of the couch.

The rain had stopped as Ellen reached down through the window and clasped Tanya's hand, but it didn't change the fact that Ellen could not lift Tanya the ten inches or so that Tanya needed to reach the window ledge. Not only was she still sore from gravedigging, but she didn't have the strength to lift Tanya.

"Pull, Ellen," Tanya begged.

"Can you jump up to reach the ledge?" Ellen asked.

Tanya jumped but not high enough. "I'm too scared I'll fall and break my neck."

Just then, Ellen felt her phone vibrate in her pocket. "Hold on. That might be Nora." Ellen released Tanya's hand to check the text. "It is. She's wondering where I am. I'll tell her I have a flat tire and have to reschedule."

Ellen sent the text, returned her phone to her pants' pocket, and said, "Is there anything down there you can put on the back of the couch, to boost you up?"

Tanya left the window to have a look around the basement. The black cat had disappeared.

"She might have to go out another way," Sue said. "Why don't you try those sliding glass doors to the backyard?"

"What if I set off an alarm?" Tanya pointed out.

Sue glanced at Ellen. "We might not have a choice."

Another set of headlights appeared on the street. Sue killed the flashlight again. The vehicle slowed down in front of Nora's house.

"That can't be Nora already," Ellen murmured.

"No way," Tanya said.

"No." Sue crouched down on her hands and knees behind Ellen. "It's not Nora. It's a taxicab."

"A taxicab?" Tanya repeated.

"Someone's getting out of it and walking up to the house," Sue added. "It's a young woman."

"She has red, curly hair," Ellen observed, wondering if this might be Nora's daughter.

"Oh, mother trucker!" Tanya cried. "What if she has a key?"

"Shh, listen," Ellen said. "She's talking to someone on the phone."

"Hey, Mom . . . Yes, I'm at your house now . . . the flight was fine . . . yes . . . okay, but what's the garage code again? . . . Okay . . . thanks . . . See you soon."

The young woman waved the cabby off and dragged her rolling luggage up the driveway to the garage door, where she entered a code into the keypad. The garage door opened.

"Oh, Tanya," Ellen cried. "You need to get out of there now!"

Tanya found a foot stool and wedged it onto the back of the couch. Then she jumped like a cat from the stool to the cat door, pulling herself up and out. The foot stool fell to the basement floor with a clatter.

"Are you okay?" Sue asked Tanya.

"I bumped my head and scraped my back," Tanya said as she climbed to her feet. "Come on. Let's get out of here."

Ellen followed Tanya with the tote full of Dan's ashes but tripped on a tree root and fell to her hands and knees. The tote dropped to the ground, too, and fell on its side. Ellen gasped, more concerned with the ashes than with the pain from the fall. Fortunately, only a tiny bit of the ash had spilled onto the ground. Ellen scooped it up, along with some mud—to make sure she had gotten it all—and then Sue helped her to her feet.

"Come on," Sue urged. "Lights are turning on inside. We can't risk being spotted out here."

Tanya was long gone, already waiting in the vehicle. If she'd had the key, she could have picked up Sue and Ellen, who had no choice but to hobble across the front lawn in the bright light of the streetlamp and two houses down to the Rogue. Once they were in the vehicle, Sue punched the pedal and sped off.

"Geez Louise, that was close!" Ellen cried.

"Tell me about it," Sue said with a laugh.

When Tanya made no comment, Ellen leaned forward in her seat. "You okay?"

"All that trouble, and we don't even know if we have the right ashes."

"But physically you're okay, right?" Sue asked. "Or are you hurt?"

"I'm okay. Ugh! I can't believe I let you two talk me into that. It was so stressful!"

"Just think about the good you're doing," Ellen reminded her. "You're helping so many people. Dan can rest, and the tribe can have their land back, unencumbered by a vengeful ghost."

"If we have the right ashes," Tanya said.

"We have the right ashes," Sue said.

Tanya shook her head. "You don't know that."

"Let's operate under the assumption that we do," Ellen suggested. "And just give it our best try, okay?"

"Don't you think I'm doing that? That was my best try, Ellen. I nearly killed myself climbing out of there."

"Tell me what I can do to make you feel better," Sue said to Tanya.

"I want pasta," Tanya said. "I want a big plate of fettucine smothered in alfredo sauce with soft French bread and a Caesar salad."

"That's not specific," Sue teased with a laugh.

"I'll order us takeout from The Pink Door!" Ellen exclaimed. "We can take it back to the room and celebrate our *assumed* victory."

"Now that's the best idea I've heard all day," Tanya said.

Sue chuckled. "I think I can live with that decision, too."

So much for skipping a meal, Ellen thought with a smile.

Once they had their food and had parked the car and were about to leave the Rogue to enter the Hyatt Regency, Tanya said to Ellen, "You're not bringing those ashes in with us, are you? Why not leave them in the car?"

Ellen, who had strapped the tote over her shoulder, replied, "I don't want to risk something happening to them."

"Like what?" Sue challenged. "You think someone's going to steal a tote full of dirt?"

"I do not want to sleep in the same hotel room with the ashes of a ghost that tried to kill us," Tanya complained. "Come on, Ellen. Leave them in the car."

"Fine." Ellen tucked the tote onto the floorboard behind the driver's seat and, with Moseby on his leash, followed her friends inside.

CHAPTER TWENTY

Return to Quillayute Prairie

E arly Friday morning after a quick breakfast in the hotel, Ellen and her friends, along with her little dog Mo, piled into the Nissan Rogue and headed back to Quillayute Prairie Cemetery, where they would finally reunite the ashes—or what they hoped were the ashes—of Dan Pullen with his grave.

Once they were on the road, Ellen, feeling lighter in spirit, maybe because the sun was shining, or maybe because she felt hopeful about bringing peace to the ghost, said to her friends from the back seat, "I think I'll call Mary Pullen to give her an update."

"Good idea," Sue said from behind the wheel. "Do y'all mind if I stop for a cherry coke at the next Sonic?"

"Of course not," Tanya said. "I'll get a small Dr. Pepper. I don't like to drink soda, because it bothers my bladder, but I need a pick-me-up."

Sue looked at Ellen in the rearview mirror. "You want anything?"

Ellen, who had already dialed Mary's number, shook her head just as Mary was answering the call.

"Hi, Mary. It's Ellen McManius. I have an update for you regarding Dan Pullen's remains."

Ellen caught Mary up to speed but was disappointed by the librarian-shaman's reaction. Ellen had expected the woman to be over the moon.

"I hope it works," Mary said.

"Why wouldn't it?" Ellen hadn't mentioned that there was a chance they had the wrong ashes.

"I'm putting her on speaker," Tanya said.

"Cremations are tricky. The spirit often attaches itself to an object when the remains are destroyed."

Ellen had planned to be cremated herself. Paul had wanted a traditional burial, but Ellen wanted her ashes to be spread over Paul's grave. Brian had seemed okay with her wishes when he said he'd have his ashes spread there, too, and they'd be a threesome for all eternity.

"Why wouldn't the spirit move on and find peace after cremation?" Ellen wondered.

"Most do," Mary said. "But those that choose to remain on the earth must bind themselves to a physical object when their remains aren't an option."

"Do you think that's what Dan's ghost has done?" Sue asked. "Has he attached himself to the bungalow?"

"Not the bungalow, because it wasn't built until the thirties. He had to have attached himself to an object that was already around at the time of his death."

"The silverware," Ellen speculated. "Do you know if it's Hattie's?"

"I think so," Mary replied.

"Could he have attached to an entire set?" Sue asked.

"Possibly," Mary said. "If so, the silverware will need to be salted and destroyed for the ghost to leave the hill."

"How do you destroy silverware?" Tanya wondered.

"You can't really destroy silver," Mary said, "but you can melt the silverware down, salt it, and bury it. Just the process of melting it with a butane torch might be enough to drive out the ghost."

Ellen lifted her brows. "That sounds like a lot of work."

"You'd obviously want a degree of certainty first," Mary explained. "He might not be bound to the silverware. It might be Hattie's painting of the original house."

"Oh, true," Ellen said. "So how can we know?"

"Aren't you paranormal investigators?"

Ellen and her friends exchanged glances.

"Well, yes, but we're supposed to fly out tomorrow," Tanya said.

"We'll talk it over," Ellen quickly added, "and get back with you."

"Are you staying in the bungalow tonight? Or have you vacated the premises?"

"We've vacated," Sue said. "Though we left a lot of things behind. I hope you understand why."

"Didn't you hear about the windows?" Tanya asked.

"Yes. Jackson cleaned up the mess and covered the windows with tarpaulins in case you still wanted to stay there."

Sue and Tanya laughed.

"No way," Tanya said adamantly.

"But we might be open to an investigation," Ellen said. "We'll call you back."

Ellen ended the call and leaned forward in her seat. "What do you think, guys? We've gone this far. Shouldn't we see it through to the end? My equipment is still in the bungalow, and I wouldn't mind getting it back."

"We've never dealt with a ghost that was this aggressive," Tanya pointed out. "Even the Shinigami wasn't this terrifying."

"It would feel good to help the tribe," Sue said in a contemplative tone. "Wouldn't it, Tanya?"

"Of course, it would."

"Let's think about it," Ellen said. "We don't have to decide anything this second."

Sue pulled into a Sonic, where they each got a drink before they continued their drive to the Quillayute Prairie Cemetery.

"Someone's at the gravesite," Tanya pointed out as Sue pulled onto the side of the road near the cemetery three and a half hours after they'd left Seattle. "Are those reporters? What are they doing?"

"Give me your binoculars." Sue motioned to Tanya.

"Ellen, they're in the back. Can you reach them?"

Ellen unstrapped her seatbelt, climbed onto her knees, careful to avoid Moseby's tail, and searched around the cargo area, where a pillow, blanket, two jackets, and the plastic tub of grout lay strewn across the bottom. "I don't see them. Oh, wait. Here they are."

Ellen handed them over to Sue, who pressed them to her eyes.

"Oh, my gawd. It's Nora and her daughter. That must be Nora's Honda Pilot parked on the other side of the road. See it? Nora is holding the brass urn, and there's dust in the air over the grave. I think she just poured the gray grout on Dan Pullen's grave."

"Ugh!" Tanya cried. "I risked my life for nothing!"

"We couldn't have known," Ellen said. "And hey, at least we know we have the right ashes."

Tanya sighed. "I'll admit that's a relief. Oh, gosh. Why didn't Nora tell us that she was planning to do this?"

Sue continued to watch through the binoculars. "She didn't think it was any of our business."

"She might not have decided to do it until after we left," Ellen pointed out. "We probably guilted her into it."

Tanya shrugged. "Or maybe her daughter talked her into it."

"Oh no, they're coming this way." Sue handed the binoculars to Tanya. "Let's get out of here and come back later."

Ellen and Tanya ducked down in the seats as Sue drove.

"They can't see you," Sue said with a laugh. "They're too far away."

Tanya sat up. "I guess you're right."

Once Sue had driven a half a mile or so from the cemetery and they were out of sight of Nora and her daughter, Ellen asked, "Is anyone hungry? Why don't we grab some lunch and come back to the grave after?"

"I like the sound of that," Sue said cheerfully.

"I want garlic fries from River's Edge," Tanya said.

Sue shook her head. "Well, I guess the birthday girl gets what the birthday girl wants."

After the young waitress had taken their order at the restaurant in La Push, she cocked her head to the side and asked, "By any chance, are you the ladies staying at the enchanted bungalow?"

"Not anymore," Sue said.

"I heard about you at drum circle the other night. Thank you for helping us."

"We haven't done much," Ellen pointed out.

"Not true," the young woman—probably early twenties—replied. "Now that we know he's not buried there, we have a chance of breaking the curse."

Ellen glanced nervously at her friends, feeling a wave of guilt overcome her. They hadn't exactly done all they could.

"We hope we helped, if even a little bit," Tanya said, her face slightly pink.

"I'm going to ask my manager to comp your meals."

"No, don't do that," Sue insisted. "We want to pay."

The young woman gave her a smile but appeared intent on doing it anyway. "I'll be back soon with your order."

Once the waitress had left the table, Ellen said, her voice lowered, "Guys, we need to finish the job."

Tanya sipped at her hot tea, and Sue gazed out the window at the seals playing in the river, which sparkled in the sunlight. Even Moseby avoided eye contact.

"It's our calling," Ellen insisted. "How many times have we said we were going to quit only to be pulled back in. This is what we're meant to do. We're good at it. Think how many people we've helped."

"True," Sue agreed. "We are good at. We do have the gift—not just me, but all of us."

"Y'all are just going to gang up on me again, until I give in, so why don't we skip that part?"

Ellen shook her head. "Not this time. This is your birthday trip. You come first this time."

"This *one* time," Sue teased.

"Great, now I feel selfish," Tanya grumbled. "You know I want to help the tribe. I just don't want to die doing it."

"You're right," Ellen said. "It's too risky. Let's just forget it and enjoy the rest of the trip."

"I know you don't mean that," Tanya said, exasperated. "I can tell when you're using reverse psychology on me."

Ellen and Sue laughed.

Ellen said, "Gosh, we know each other so well, don't we? We know all each other's tricks."

The friends laughed—including Tanya.

"I have an idea," Sue blurted out suddenly. "What if we offer to investigate on the condition that Mary and a couple of Quileute police officers are there, too, for extra protection?"

"That's a good idea," Ellen agreed.

"It's the only way I'll do it," Tanya said as the food was being brought to their table.

"Does that mean you're in?" Sue asked Tanya.

Tanya took a bite of her garlic fries. "Let's think about it while we eat."

The cemetery was empty an hour later when Sue pulled the Rogue onto the side of the road. Ellen hopped out with Moseby on his leash and with the tote of Dan's ashes draped over her shoulder. It was a gorgeous day—the blue sky clearer than every day since she'd arrived.

As they strolled toward the grave, Tanya said, "We should scrape up the grout, shouldn't we? What will happen to it after it rains? Won't it get thick, like cement?"

"I hadn't thought of that," Sue said. "Do we have an empty bag to put it in?"

"We have the plastic tub of grout in the back of the Rogue," Ellen said. "Mo and I will go back for it and meet you there."

"Give me the ashes, then," Tanya offered.

Ellen handed the tote over, and then she and Moseby returned to the Rogue for the plastic container of grout. When Ellen caught up to her friends, she found them bent over, raking the gray grout from the top of the grave with their fingers. As she bent over to do the same, Ellen wondered if the dirt had been returned to the grave by cemetery staff or the Quileute police.

With most of the grout collected, Ellen and Tanya stood on opposite sides of the grave, each holding a strap of the tote. Then they tilted the bag and sprinkled the ashes from the top to the bottom of the grave, going for an even distribution that resembled what Nora had done with the grout.

"Shouldn't we say something?" Sue asked.

"I guess so," Ellen said.

Tanya handed the empty tote to Ellen. "Go for it, Sue."

Sue cleared her throat. "We pray to God for the peaceful repose of Dan Pullen's soul. May he rest in peace."

"May he rest in peace," Ellen echoed.

Tanya wiped a tear from her eye. "May he rest in peace."

Ellen studied her tall friend. "Are you crying, Tanya?"

"Not really. Just a little. I know he did some bad things, but he had good in him, too. I hope he can find peace."

"Does this mean you've made a decision?" Sue asked.

Ellen held her breath, trying not to get her hopes up.

"I have a proposition for you," Tanya began.

Ellen crossed her arms at her chest. "We're listening."

"If you can get Mary and a couple of police officers to join us, and if you drive me to Sekiu Point first to look for whales, then I'll help with the investigation."

Ellen and Sue smiled at one another and said, simultaneously, "Deal."

CHAPTER TWENTY-ONE

A Paranormal Investigation

Dusk had just blanketed the Pacific, and after a gorgeous day, it was only now beginning to rain when Ellen and her friends arrived at the enchanted bungalow and pulled up behind the black pickup truck already parked there. Waiting outside near the truck were Officers Hobucket and Pullen and Mary Pullen. The tribal council had agreed to permit them to break the ban on entering the property because it was in the best interest of the tribe to do so.

"You stay in the car, Moseby-Mo," Ellen said to her dog before climbing from the Nissan Rogue.

Although Ellen and her friends hadn't spotted any whales at Sekiu, they had observed the sea lions again when they came to feed at the marina during high tide.

On the way back to La Push, Tanya had asked if they could stop north of the Quillayute River to stretch their legs on Rialto Beach.

Sue had said, "You have the upper hand, and you're going to milk it for as long as you can."

Tanya had laughed but hadn't denied it.

Nevertheless, Sue and Ellen had enjoyed the spontaneous adventure, for by the time they'd reached the beach, the sun was beginning to set, and the tide, though not low, was on its way out, leaving behind all manner of sea life in the tide pools. They saw gorgeous starfish and sea anemone in every color, and other creatures they couldn't even identify.

Though they saw no orcas, it had been a pleasant walk. Moseby had liked it, too.

Now it was time to do the investigation they were all dreading but felt called to do.

Officers Hobucket and Pullen led the group over the threshold of the enchanted bungalow, and Ellen, who took up the rear, announced, "We come in peace."

Sue added, "Dan Pullen, we spread your ashes on your grave on the Quillayute Prairie and prayed to God for the peaceful repose of your soul. We aren't your enemy."

Ellen glanced at Mary, who frowned.

Well, at least some of them weren't his enemy, she thought.

"It's possible that he's not here, right?" Tanya whispered. "He may have moved on."

"I can feel him," Mary revealed. "He's still here, along with all his hate and negativity."

Ellen shuddered. She felt it, too, but hadn't wanted to believe it.

"Let's set up the equipment." Ellen crossed the room to one of her full-spectrum cameras. "Let's point one camera toward the fireplace and painting, a second toward the kitchen and silverware, and the third toward the bathroom and stairwell, since those are the main areas of activity."

"Can I help you with that?" Officer Hobucket offered to Tanya as she attempted to carry one of the cameras across the room.

"That would be awesome, thank you. I'm still so sore from digging."

"I'll take some initial readings of temperature and electro-magnetic frequencies," Sue volunteered.

"I don't think we want to use the EMF generator," Tanya said. "The ghost has enough power as it is."

"I agree," Ellen said as she finished checking her cameras. "No candles either."

Ellen was glad that she hadn't had to abandon her equipment. Her full-spectrum cameras, which could see and capture normal, infrared, ultraviolet, and other types of light images, weren't cheap or easy to find. They were especially helpful at pin-pointing infrared images of what ghost hunters believed to be human spirits. The spirit images were even shaped like human bodies—or stick figures of human bodies. If Dan Pullen were possessing an object in the bungalow, one of the cameras might be able to reveal which object it was.

"These cameras work better without the lights on," Ellen said. "Would you mind if we conduct the investigation in the dark?"

"We expected that," Officer Hobucket shared. "This isn't our first paranormal rodeo."

"That's a relief," Sue replied as she helped Ellen turn off the lights.

Even with the lights off, the bungalow and its occupants were visible as moonlight washed in through the big picture window.

"I'd like to use something called the Estes Method," Mary said.

"Is that an ancient tribal custom?" Sue asked.

"No. It's a technique I learned from Youtube."

Ellen wasn't sure if Mary was being sarcastic or serious as the two police officers glanced at one another and chuckled, so she said nothing.

"How does it work?" Tanya asked.

Mary stretched her hand out to her grandson, who unhooked a pair of earphones with antennae from his belt and handed them to her.

"These shuffle through radio channels," Mary explained. "It's a way of asking a ghost to communicate with us."

"Like a ghost box," Ellen said.

"Exactly. I'll blindfold myself, and together with the earphones, block out other stimuli. One of you will ask questions, questions that I won't be able to hear, and we can see if my answers make sense. This way I won't be influenced by your questions."

"I see," Sue said. "This ought to be interesting."

"We should also keep our eyes on the bathroom mirror and the picture window," Ellen said to the police officers. "The ghost has written messages to us in both places."

"Turn on the hot water in the bathroom," Mary suggested.

"I'll do it," Jackson offered.

Once the equipment was set up, the circle of salt poured, and the initial readings taken, Mary sat in the rocking chair near the hearth with a bandana tied over her eyes and the headphones over her ears. She began to rock back and forth, her head bobbing, as if in a trance.

"Who wants to start?" Ellen asked the others.

"I'll go." Sue cleared her throat. "Dan Pullen, as I said, we come in peace. Our goal is to help you move on, so your soul can finally rest. To do that, we want to know where you are. Are you here? Can you talk to us?"

"Yes," Mary confirmed. "I'm here."

The floor lamp beside Ellen flickered on and off. Ellen and Tanya exchanged anxious looks.

"Okay, good," Sue continued. "Thank you."

"Wait," Mary said. "Who are they?"

"I am Sue Graham, a paranormal investigator," Sue introduced herself.

"The others," Mary said.

"These are my co-investigators, Tanya Sanchez and Ellen McManius."

"The others," Mary said again.

"We are joined by three members of the Quileute tribe: Officers Hobucket and Pullen, and a shaman named Mary Pullen. She's the one who is channeling you."

"No," Mary insisted.

"No?" Sue repeated. "What do you mean?"

"Not friends," Mary said. "Not my friends."

"Yes, they are," Sue assured the ghost, even if it might have been a lie. "We are all your friends. We are here to help."

"I hate," Mary said, then she added, "them."

"They didn't do anything to you, Dan," Sue reasoned. "They aren't the people who fought with you over your land. Those Quileute are long gone."

"No, they aren't. I see them."

"You see them?" Sue repeated.

"On the beach," Mary said.

Sue glanced at Ellen, and Ellen shrugged.

"How . . .ee . . . cattle," Mary added. "I see him just outside. My enemy."

"Howeattle," Tanya whispered. "The one he killed."

"Yes," Mary said.

Ellen glanced around the moonlit room. "Mary and these officers are not your enemies. They aren't the spirits on the beach. They are their descendants, like Nora Phillips is yours. Do you know Nora? We met her this week. She's your great-granddaughter. She and her daughter visited your grave. They have Hattie's red hair."

"Love," Mary said. "My love."

"Hattie was your love, right?" Sue asked.

"Yes. My love."

"Do you know Nora?" Ellen asked again. "Do you know your great-granddaughter, who looks like Hattie?"

"No."

"Do you remember your children?" Sue asked. "Do you remember Mildred, Dee, Royal, and Chester?"

"Dolly," Mary said. "We called her . . . Dolly."

Ellen's brows shot up. If she hadn't been certain they were speaking with Daniel Pullen, there was no doubt now—unless Mary really could hear them and was making it all up.

"That's right," Sue said. "Dolly. So, you remember your children?"

"My loves."

"They are resting in peace, Dan," Ellen said. "Wouldn't you like to join them on the other side?"

"Stuck."

"He's trapped here," Tanya whispered.

"Yes," Mary said. "Long time. Forever."

"Go away," Mary added.

"Do you want us to leave?" Ellen asked.

"Yes."

"Why?" Sue pressed. "Why do you want us to leave?"

"Hate," Mary said. "Violence is my only . . ."

"You're only what, Dan?" Sue asked. "Violence is your only what?"

"Salvation," Mary said.

"It doesn't have to be that way," Sue promised. "We can help you to get unstuck."

"Go," Mary said again.

"Tell us where you are," Ellen demanded. "Are you in Hattie's painting?"

"Love," Mary said.

"Are you in her painting?" Sue repeated.

"No."

"Are you possessing Hattie's silverware?" Ellen asked.

"Go . . . now."

"We aren't leaving until you tell us where you are," Sue insisted.

"Dee," Mary said.

"What about Dee?" Sue asked. "Are you talking about your son?"

"Yes. He . . . showed me."

"Showed you what, Dan?" Ellen asked.

"A way."

Sue glanced at Ellen. "A way to what?"

"Stay," Mary said. "Showed me . . . a way."

"What way?" Sue asked.

Mary remained silent for many seconds.

Ellen asked, "Don't you want to be with Dee and your other children and Hattie? Don't you want to move on to the other side?"

"I don't know," Mary said. "Not mine."

"Oh," Tanya whispered. "He's afraid Hattie will reject him on the other side."

"Yes," Mary said. "Not my . . . Hat . . . ee."

"Things are different on the other side," Ellen reassured the ghost. "When you're with God, all the petty hurts and jealousies go away, and all that's left is love—pure love. Dan, Hattie and all your loved ones will accept you if you'll just allow yourself to cross over. Look for a bright light filled with warmth and joy. No one will turn you away if you go with a pure heart."

"Stuck," Mary said again. "Go away."

"I pray that God and all the heavenly angels help the spirit of Dan Pullen to cross over," Sue said. "If you're a loved one of Dan Pullen's, please show him the way."

"Trapped!" Mary shouted.

Suddenly, a spoon lifted from the floor and jumped through the air toward Sue but halted in the air just outside of the circle before falling with a thud to the floor.

"I'm trying to help you, Dan!" Sue complained. "Why are you attacking me?"

"Go!" Mary said.

More silverware lifted from the floor and was hurled through the space. A butter knife landed close to Mary and slid on the floor across the circle, hitting her foot. She pulled off her blindfold to see what had touched her.

"We better take a break," Officer Hobucket advised as he glanced around at the floating silverware.

Mary removed the headphones. "What did you say, Ahmik?"

"Let's take a break," he repeated. "Before things get out of hand."

"I'll turn off the water," Jackson offered.

"Grab a camera on the way out." Ellen took the one closest to her and headed for the front door.

The six investigators piled into their vehicles and reconvened at the library. They sat around the conference table reviewing their footage. Ellen held Mo on her lap in his cloth pooch carrier while she and Jackson watched the camera that had been pointing toward the bathroom. Ellen had focused the lens on the entire stairwell just in case it picked up anything on the stairs—since she had suspected the ghost had found his way up into the loft.

Sue and Officer Hobucket reviewed the coverage of the kitchen, and Tanya and Mary looked over the video of Mary rocking before the fireplace, Hattie's painting just overhead on the mantle.

"Do you see anything that resembles a stickperson?" Ellen asked the others.

"Not yet," Sue said.

"Nothing here either," Tanya said.

"Wait a minute." Jackson pointed to the eight-inch-by-eight-inch screen Ellen held in her hands. "What's that?"

Ellen squinted through her readers. To the left of the bathroom door was a smaller door that led to the short closet beneath the stairs—the one that Ellen had decided not to clean because it had too many cobwebs. On the video, a stick figure seemed to be crawling through the closet door.

"Oh my gosh!" Ellen whispered.

"What do you see?" Sue wanted to know.

But Ellen couldn't speak. She was transfixed by the movements of the stick figure. One "foot" remained on the door while the rest of the figure stretched the length of the living room, stopping at the edge of the circle of protection.

Sue got up from her chair to stand beside Ellen. Soon the others gathered behind Ellen and Jackson to watch the footage. Ellen rewound the video, so they could see the stick man as he stretched from the tiny closet door across the room.

"He's in there," Mary said. "He must be attached to something inside that closet."

"Do you know if any of the materials from the original house were used to build the bungalow?" Sue asked.

"They burned the original house," Officer Hobucket said.

"That's right," Mary confirmed. "The bungalow was completely new."

Officer Pullen scratched his chin. "There could be some old equipment, an old broom, or something like that that made its way into the new bungalow from the original house, right Grandma?"

"Whatever it is," Mary began, "we now know that the ghost is possessing it, thanks to this video."

Ellen nodded. "Found you, Dan Pullen. And now we're coming to get you."

CHAPTER TWENTY-TWO

Howeattle

Ellen felt hopeful and terrified as she and the other investigators returned from the library to the enchanted bungalow just before nine o'clock. The rain had stopped, but the wind was fierce on the hill where she gave Moseby a long hug before leaving him in the Rogue and following the others inside.

"We come in peace," she announced again as she crossed the threshold.

The silverware lay lifeless on the floor, glinting in the moonlight bathing the bungalow.

"I'll use that broom, if I may," Officer Hobucket said of Ellen's broom leaning against the side of the refrigerator. "The closet's a bit small to get into."

Ellen handed him the broom. "Good idea."

"Thank goodness," Tanya chuckled. "I've been anxiously waiting for my friends to ask me to crawl in there."

"We wouldn't do that," Ellen insisted.

"Yeah, right." Tanya laughed.

The officer opened the closet door, which was about three feet tall and wide.

"Oh, that smell." Sue waved a hand in front of her face.

Ellen pointed her full-spectrum camera at the opening, trying to get an image of the stick person who had stretched from the door in their earlier footage.

"Getting anything?" Mary asked Ellen.

"Not yet," Ellen answered.

The older officer pushed the broom into the closet as far as he could reach. "I might have to crawl in there after all. I don't feel anything yet."

"I'll do it," Jackson volunteered, holding his hand out for the broom. "I'm smaller than you, Ahmik. I can get back in there."

Officer Hobucket handed over the broom.

Just then the camera picked up an image of something that appeared to be crawling toward them.

Ellen gasped. "See that?"

Mary nodded.

Sue and Tanya leaned over the monitor to get a look, too.

Officer Pullen pushed the end of the broom into the dark closet and swept toward him with one smooth stroke. When that yielded nothing, he ducked and bent his legs and entered the tiny room, so he could get the broom all the way to the back.

"Ohhh!" Jackson, falling to the floor, shouted.

Tanya squealed, and Ellen covered her mouth as Jackson was suddenly dragged by his feet deeper into the closet beneath the stairs.

"Ahhh!" the officer shrieked.

Sue took several steps back. "Oh, my gawd!"

Ellen might have peed a little.

"Jackson?" Mary cried. "You alright?"

Officer Hobucket knelt on the floor and shined his flashlight into the closet. Mary, Ellen, Sue, and Tanya crouched behind Ahmik, trying to get a view of Jackson, who seemed to have disappeared. Ellen's heart was racing as she held her breath.

"Jackson?" Officer Hobucket called.

"I found something," Jackson shouted.

Ellen sighed with relief.

"Thank God," Sue whispered. "That was scary."

"Did the ghost pull you in?" Mary asked. "Does he still have a hold of you, Jackson?"

Something rolled from the dark closet and stopped at Officer Hobucket's knee.

The officer picked it up and studied it. "It's a really old baseball. A Spalding. One of the first ever made."

"Dee's baseball," Tanya whispered. "Remember what Nora said? Dee put a baseball into Pullen's empty casket."

"So, how did it get here?" Sue wanted to know.

"It has *Love, Dee* written on it," Officer Hobucket added. "It's barely legible, but it's there."

"Jackson?" Mary said again. "Are you coming out of there?"

Officer Hobucket returned his flashlight to the closet and searched for his colleague. Ellen pointed her full-spectrum camera at it, too.

Jackson finally emerged covered in cobwebs. As he climbed to his feet, Ellen gasped. The camera revealed the stickperson reaching from the baseball in Ahmik's hand toward the younger officer, whose skin had paled and whose eyes had a tinge of red in them.

"Jackson, get away from that baseball!" Ellen warned. "I think Pullen's trying to attach to you!"

The ball dropped from Ahmik's hand and rolled to Jackson's feet. Jackson fell to the ground again, and he and the ball slid across the floor back toward the tiny closet.

Ellen and her friends screamed.

Mary and Tanya grabbed Jackson's hands while Ahmik went for the baseball. The ball evaded Ahmik, who dropped on his hands and knees and crawled into the closet after it. Ellen kept the full-spectrum camera fixed on them as Sue took Ahmik's abandoned flashlight and shined it on the struggling Quileute.

"He's still trying to climb into Jackson's body!" Ellen warned.

"I got the ball!" Ahmik cried as he backed out of the tiny opening.

Then the officer threw the ball into the hearth. On her camera, Ellen saw the stick figure fly with the ball through the air, and she was relieved that the younger officer was finally out of danger. But now a second stick figure emerged from the picture window.

"What's that?" Ellen said pointing to her monitor.

The officers climbed to their feet and joined Ellen and the others around the camera monitor. The stick figure at the window raised its arms, and, with a woosh, fire ignited the old, ashen logs in the hearth. They shouldn't have been able to catch flame, but they did.

"It's Howeattle," Mary said. "I can see him. He speaks to me."

"What's he saying?" Officer Pullen asked.

"It's done," Mary said jubilantly. "The ghost of Dan Pullen is gone!"

"Really?" Tanya asked.

"The fire in the hearth has released his ghost," Mary explained.

Ellen and her friends clapped their hands with glee.

"Thank goodness!" Sue shouted merrily.

"What a relief!" Tanya said.

"Let's add salt to the fire, just in case," Ellen suggested.

"I'll do it," Jackson offered. He grabbed the cannister from where Ellen had left it on the kitchen counter before shaking some into the flames.

"What's Howeattle doing now?" Ellen, who had been studying him on the camera monitor, asked, as the figure seemed to be dancing.

"He's celebrating," Mary observed. "He's finally won a century-old battle, and now, he, too, can find peace."

Tears pricked Ellen's eyes. "Now that's poetic justice."

"True," Sue agreed. "Dan set fire to him, and he's just set fire to Dan, but in the end, they are both at peace."

Ellen and her friends watched the dancing stick figure on the camera, the joy in its movements clear. It brought satisfaction and peace to Ellen's heart to know the old warrior could finally rest.

"Howeattle has a message for you ladies," Mary announced.

Sue's brows disappeared beneath her bangs, and Tanya's mouth dropped open.

"For us?" Ellen asked in disbelief. "He has a message *for us*?"

"He says you should take the Port Townsend/Coupeville Ferry tomorrow before continuing on to Seattle."

Ellen and her friends exchanged curious looks.

"I wonder why," Sue pondered.

"I don't know," Mary said. "He didn't explain."

"But I would do what he says," Officer Hobucket advised. "He doesn't give messages lightly."

"We certainly will!" Ellen exclaimed. "I agree that it wouldn't be wise to ignore a message from beyond."

"Are we sleeping here then?" Tanya asked Ellen and Sue with bent brows. "Our bags are in Seattle."

"It's a bit late to make the drive tonight," Sue pointed out. "Unless *you* want to drive while *I* sleep."

"No, thanks," Tanya said wryly, then, turning to Mary, asked, "Is it really safe here in the bungalow?"

"It's perfectly safe now," Mary assured her. "Add more of those logs to the fire to keep you warm, and you'll be alright."

"I just remembered something," Sue said with a grin. "Tanya's leftover birthday cake is still in the fridge. Who's ready for a nighttime snack?"

"Me!" Ellen said gleefully. "I'll get Moseby from the car. He'll be happy to stretch his legs."

Ellen set her camera on the kitchen bar and rushed out to the car for her pup. She leashed him and took him for a walk around to the back of the bungalow, where a nearly full moon hovered over the sea, illuminating the waves crashing against the hillside below. That first night Ellen had arrived ten days ago, a new moon had made it impossible to see the ocean at night, and she had felt small and nervous below the glittering stars. Now, with the bright moon smiling down on her, and the splendid view of the sea below, she felt content. She could only imagine how restless the ghosts of Dan Pullen and Howeattle had been during their century-long battle for this hilltop, and she was so very grateful to have played a small part in bringing that suffering to an end.

After a peaceful night's sleep in the bungalow, Ellen and her friends loaded Ellen's equipment into the Rogue and, together with Moseby, drove the scenic route toward the Port Townsend/Coupeville Ferry. Along the way, they stopped in Port Angeles at Bella Italia for another plate of Bella's mushroom ravioli, which was a nice way to bid adieu to their *Twilight* tour. Then, after waiting in line for the ferry, they drove aboard, parked, and climbed out of their vehicle. Ellen carried Moseby in his cloth pooch carrier, and she and her three friends stood together at the rail with the wind blowing their hair away from their faces. Tanya had her binoculars because she hadn't given up her hope of seeing an orca.

As she stood with the binoculars pressed to her face, Tanya said, "Thank you guys for giving me the best birthday ever."

"Was it really the best ever?" Sue asked.

"It ranks right up there." Tanya smiled. "This area is so beautiful, and the walks and the hiking were so much fun. Forks was fun, too. And the bungalow, its views, it was all so amazing."

"The ghost of Dan Pullen didn't ruin it for you?" Ellen needled. "Be honest."

"Had things ended differently, it might have. But no, I feel so good about what we accomplished. We did it again, girls!"

"It feels good, doesn't it." Sue noted without inflection.

"Let's plan another trip," Tanya suggested. "Maybe over the holidays. I want to go someplace Christmassy."

Sue took out her phone. "I'm asking Google what the most Christmassy town in America is."

Ellen threw her head back and laughed. "Good ol' Google, that bard of wisdom."

"Williamsburg, Virginia," Sue began. "That's interesting. My mom always said that one of her favorite places to visit was Colonial Williamsburg, except that every time she walked the historical streets, she sensed someone following her—someone not of this world."

"Did she ever find out what it was?" Ellen asked.

"Uh-uh. She used to call him the Virginia Creeper."

"Like the vine?" Tanya clarified. "The poisonous one?"

"Yeah, that was the joke." Sue's expression turned thoughtful. "You know Mom. She was always trying to be funny."

"Like mother like daughter," Ellen teased with a smile.

"I've heard that Busch Gardens are gorgeous over the holidays," Tanya said. "We should go!"

"Count me in," Sue said. "It'll make me feel closer to my mother."

"Maybe we'll even meet her Virginia Creeper," Ellen said with a laugh.

"Oh, I can't believe it!" Tanya said, still holding the binoculars to her face. "Oh, wow! It's an Orca! Can you see it? Make that two!"

Ellen gazed out at the ocean and saw the two giant whales spouting water before flipping their tails through the air.

"Aw! I'm so glad you got to see them for your birthday!" Sue cheered.

"Moseby, can you see the orcas?" Ellen said sweetly to her dog.

Moseby barked and licked her cheek.

"Will Moseby be joining us in Williamsburg?" Sue asked.

"What do you think, Moseby-Mo?" Ellen asked. "You want to go with Mama and her friends to Williamsburg?"

Moseby barked and licked her cheek again and squirmed to get out of his carrier.

Ellen took him out so he could feel the wind through his fur, and they watched the orcas follow the ferry all the way to the next port.

"This is why Howeattle wanted us to go this route," Tanya realized suddenly. "He knew how badly we wanted to see the orcas."

***

THE END

Thank you for reading my story. I hope you enjoyed it! If you did, please consider leaving a review. Reviews help other readers to discover my books, which helps me.

Please visit my website at evapohler.com to get the next book, *Virginia Creeper.*

EVA POHLER

Eva Pohler is a *USA Today* bestselling author of over thirty novels in multiple genres, including mysteries, thrillers, and young adult paranormal romance based on Greek mythology. Her books have been described as "addictive" and "sure to thrill"—*Kirkus Reviews*.

To learn more about Eva and her books, and to sign up to hear about new releases and sales, please visit her website at https://www.evapohler.com.